I dialed 911. The phone was dead.

All the other phones had no dial tone either.

I couldn't believe it. The storm hadn't seemed *that* bad. No electrical storms, no raging winds to tear down lines, just falling snow. The fuel oil furnace and the phones both? But Tess had complained about the phone lines going down in a bad thunderstorm during the summer. Maybe it was just the weight of the snow pulling down a line.

Of course the fax and e-mail were dead since they depended on the phone lines.

My car phone! I wrapped the quilt around me again on top of the robe and shoved my double-socked feet into another pair of boots. I was changing clothes more often than a model on a catwalk.

In preparation for the snowstorm, we'd put the cars in the garage alongside the snowmobiles. As I raced toward both our cars, something seemed strange. They seemed to sit funny. What was wrong? Immediately I saw the answer . . .

About the Author

Carol Schmidt and her lover of sixteen years, Norma Hair, can now say that they live nowhere and everywhere. Along with a small menagerie, they are full-timers on the road in their fifth-wheeler RV towed by a pickup. Base camps are the 1871 country church in rural Michigan which they converted into a home and the RVing Women resort park in Apache Junction, Arizona.

Before writing novels full-time, Carol was a newspaper reporter, trade journal publishing house editor, public relations director for a UCLA-affiliated hospital, and small-business owner (*Words & Numbers* in the Silverlake district of Los Angeles, with Norma Hair). Both were active in L.A. lesbian-feminist politics and served on the state board of directors of California NOW. Carol co-founded White Women Against Racism and wrote for *The Lesbian News,* including a column, "Country Womyn/City Dyke." Her articles won three first-place awards from the National Gay and Lesbian Press Association.

Silverlake Heat and *Sweet Cherry Wine,* her previous novels in the Laney Samms series, were also published by Naiad, which has scheduled her next book, *Stop the Music,* for 1996.

CABIN FEVER

A LANEY SAMMS MYSTERY

A NOVEL OF
SUSPENSE
BY
CAROL SCHMIDT

THE NAIAD PRESS, INC.
1995

Printed in the United States of America on acid-free paper
First Edition

Edited by Christine Cassidy
Cover design by Bonnie Liss (Phoenix Graphics)
Typeset by Sandi Stancil

Library of Congress Cataloging-in-Publication Data

Schmidt, Carol, 1942–
    Cabin fever : a Laney Samms mystery / by Carol Schmidt.
        p.   cm.
    ISBN 1-56280-098-1
    I. Title.
PS3569.C51544C33   94-41090
813'.54—dc20
                                                                CIP

*This book is dedicated
to my beloved sister
Sandy.
Hey, we survived!*

"History is more or less bunk."

— Henry Ford
Chicago Tribune, May 25, 1916

PROLOGUE —
September, 1989

"It's a shame about Susan. You say she's going to law school? Isn't she a bit long in the tooth for that? It's not like she has to work, for God's sake. She didn't even want alimony, right?"

The white-haired man with skin like a lizard snapped a fuchsia bass plug on the end of the fine steel leader and cast his line into the reeds. He reeled it back in with jerks and starts, trying to imitate a thrashing butterfly or baby bird.

"Crazy, crazy, crazy," he muttered all the while, his wrinkled jowls shaking.

The plug made it back to the canoe unscathed.

Frederich Wilhelm Tessel scowled. He'd switch to worms if he had to, bring in a sure catch of perch. He had never gone back to the lodge empty-handed and he wasn't about to start now. Turning eighty didn't mean you forgot how to fish. Though it was a bit late in the year to be out on the Black River. He shivered in his navy parka.

His general irritation found a focus on his son. "Get a haircut, you look like a goddamn hippie. Ridiculous, a man your age, hair in your eyes."

He searched for his fur-lined cassock hat on his seat and then on the floor of the canoe. When he tugged it on, he could feel water that had splashed into the hat's lining creeping over his scalp like a cold octopus. Nothing was going right.

"I'm glad I've *got* hair," replied Frederich Wilhelm Tessel Jr., who preferred to be called Rick and who never used the "Wilhelm" or "Jr." at all except on papers his father drafted. Sometimes his father even put the "III" after Rick's name, though technically, since Rick's grandfather was no longer living, Rick was merely a "Jr." Rick wanted absolutely no connection to the ancestor he remembered as a total bastard, a gruff scarecrow of a man who'd as soon cuff his young grandson roundly on the ear as look at him. Though of course there was the money.

Rick tried to tuck the escaped thick red thatch, streaked with white to the point that sometimes he wondered if he looked like a barber pole, off of his forehead and back under his navy wool ski helmet.

"You take after me." The old man patted his hat

in satisfaction. His hair was thinner now, true, but it still covered his head. He glared back at his son. "Susan would have never let you go so long between haircuts."

Rick sighed at the renewed mention of his newly ex-wife. "Maybe that's why I'm doing it, Dad. She's entering law school at age fifty-one, to prove she can still do it, and I'm growing hair at age fifty-four, probably for the same reason." His bass jig lay dead in the water. And he was cold. Freezing cold.

He caught his father's astounded stare. "No, no, I'm joking. I just haven't gotten around to getting a haircut. I'll do it as soon as we get back to the Shores." Meaning Grosse Pointe Shores, the wealthiest of the five individual residential areas lumped together as Grosse Pointe on most maps. His own brick mansion was a few blocks away from the riverside estate of his father's. He wished they were home now, even if it meant he would be alone in the twenty-two-room house. It would be a good twenty degrees warmer down below.

Rick's red plaid Pendleton wool jacket was no match against the Michigan Upper Peninsula late September winds. Where his Thinsulate gloves were wet, he worried about frostbitten fingers, even though technically it wasn't even freezing yet. The temperature may indeed have read thirty-four degrees, but with wind chill it had to be about twenty.

In the Michigan spring the first days above freezing were blissful indications of the urgent need to throw off winter coats and walk bareheaded in the sun. Thirty-four would have seemed positively balmy. The same temperature in the fall brought its own additional chill, the ominous warning of things to come.

A few ice crystals clung to reeds along the shore, but the fast-moving Black River itself didn't usually freeze until around Christmas, when the seven waterfalls marking the river's swift path to Lake Superior became glistening ice cathedrals. He shivered just picturing them. His father didn't even have on gloves. Fool.

At least this would be their last fishing trip this year, panning his father's favorite quiet inlet off of the river, though Dad would probably drag him back here for hunting season in November when the deer would be in full rut. They'd seen two antlered males battling it out already on the backwoods drive up to the lodge. The old coot shouldn't be trusted with a rifle anymore.

"Make that thing dance, son. You'll never get anywhere in life just drifting along, waiting for something to happen." The father grabbed a paddle and rowed the canoe in closer to the weeds till the bottom rubbed on silt and muck and the clear water turned milky. Their boat renewed its slow drift. He repeated his cast, then switched to a green spotted plug resembling a frog.

Reluctantly Rick picked up his fishing pole. He gave a half-hearted cast that immediately caught in the reeds. He sighed again and pulled the canoe by way of his line toward the snag, where he used his Swiss Army knife to cut it loose. At least retying a set-up would keep his mind busy for a few minutes, not thinking about the mess that was his life.

"You know I changed my will the other day, now that Susan and her kids are out of the picture," the senior Tessel said. "Not that the brats were ever *in* the picture. We were never good enough for that brood," he snorted, glaring at the shoreline as if his recently exed daughter-in-law's family was lined up for his tirade. "Dirty money — hah!" Still grumbling mainly to himself, he yanked in his line and ripped off the lure, switching to a finer leader and tiny hook. "What's so bad about making money off of beer? Good, solid, honest money. Red-blooded American money. Just as good as what gets spent in that family's fancy department stores."

The red worm curled into frantic knots as he snapped it in half with his fingernail and speared one half with the hook, letting the other wriggling half squirm for cover under the damp gray moss in the Styrofoam cup.

"Anyway, since you never were allowed to adopt Susan's kids, they're not in the will anymore. They've got more money than they know what to do with, they don't need any of my filthy lucre." His face twisted with the words. "Susan's out, naturally. So the Tessel line lives or dies with you. Theodore and Charlotte aren't likely to have any little Tessels, that's for sure."

The old man snorted again, then snapped a red bobbin onto his line and tossed the worm bundle overboard. The bobbin just sat there. Not even a nibble. He turned back to his son.

"Naturally I made provisions for them. Theodore gets all the Key West property, since he loves Faggot

City so much. He might as well run it totally into the ground. I never liked that condo complex anyway. Too flashy. Too hot."

Rick agreed, but he still would have rather been in Florida at the moment.

"Say, son, you don't really think Theodore is, you know . . ." The old man crooked his little finger.

Of course Teddie was gay, Rick reflected. Everybody else knew it from the day he'd taken his first steps, directly toward a bouquet of lavender French lilacs on the marble coffee table. The toddler had inhaled the heady scent, sneezed, then giggled and clutched both hands to his breast in a swoon he couldn't have learned from anybody. Whenever Rick heard people debate whether gays are born or made, he remembered that moment.

Their mother had snatched Theodore away and sat him down in a pile of Tonka toy trucks, where he'd pouted. "Red-blooded American male," Rick said aloud. And so Theodore was. Rick hoped someday Theodore would come out on his own to his parents, but Rick wasn't going to be the one responsible for *that* brouhaha.

"Good, good. He just needs to find the right girl." The senior Tessel's mind wandered, then snapped back. "Oh, and I set up another trust for the Immaculate Heart of Mary nuns, so Charlotte will never be poor in her old age the way so many nuns are today. Fucking church, treating the good sisters that way, not even paying their Social Security and Medicare so they have to go on welfare."

He growled in the direction of another piece of shoreline, as if the entire Catholic Church were lined up for his disdain. "Not the IHMs anyway. Their

6

motherhouse will be a goddamn resort when I get through with it. And Charlotte can take a million dollars with her when she leaves, if she ever comes to her senses. Oh hell, probably good she stays there, says a few prayers for her old dad. Only way I'm gonna get to heaven, if there is such a place. At my age, I'd better hope there's something. If there is, your mother's there. I'll be happy. She'll make sure of that."

He glared at his placid bobbin, then at his son. Rick made some half-hearted casts under his father's baleful eye. Tessel Senior wound in the perch set-up — "Goddamn perch are sissy fish anyway" — and put on another bass lure. Rudy would hide a laugh at the sight of the two men coming in with a few dinky perch, if they even got any. There was a fat, scrappy, dinner-sized bass out there somewhere, just waiting. Usually bass bit like mad in the cold. There hadn't been many trout in recent years so he wouldn't even bother trying flies.

His anger-driven cast took out almost his whole line. The imitation crawfish in neon yellow with fluorescent green polka dots landed with a kerplunk, out of sight on the other side of a half-submerged log. Ought to be a bass there.

The old man continued, "You're still young yet. You can do anything you want with the rest of your life. The foundation just about runs itself, and what needs attention, Hank takes care of. You could have another career, another family, if you wanted. When I'm gone."

"You just said Susan was too old for law school. I'm three years older, but I can do anything?"

The senior Tessel glared at him. Never did his

son backtalk. "No, you're, you're what? Fifty-four? It's not impossible. You could marry some fine young thing and start a proper family of your own. In fact, I've been having this feeling, this intuition. You're going to meet somebody real soon, son, and I'm going to have me a grandson."

The imaginary wife and precious bundle must have been standing by the pine tree on the shore where he was staring, smiling fondly at the illusion of the model family.

He brushed aside his son's protestations. "A man can hope, can't he? Anyway, my lawyer kept insisting on some survival clause in the will, something in case you didn't survive me, God forbid. It was standard, he said. So I took the opportunity to put in a bit where any heir of yours would get everything Theodore and Charlotte didn't, if you weren't alive. Just in case, mind you."

"Dad . . ."

". . . and if there were no heirs, then everything goes to the foundation. Just so you know. I hate to keep changing that gol-darn thing. Makes me nervous. Like I'm dancing one step ahead of the devil. Which some people would say I am. Charlotte and your mother better be praying up a storm."

Rick shifted on the narrow wooden seat. He didn't like thinking about death any more than his father did. And why did he put up with this shit? Was he going to let his father go to his grave without ever once having stood up to him? Really stood up? Susan always said he never would.

Was the canoe drifting faster? He reached for the paddle to keep them in the safe inlet. Was it time to finally tell him? What the hell — the chill wind was giving him an earache. Maybe the news would get them back to the lodge early, fish or not. Maybe then they'd catch a quick shuttle flight back to City Airport and then home to his own bed.

Maybe his father was right — maybe it wasn't too late for him to start over. Without ties to the Tessel Foundation, if need be. He had a couple million in his own name in the bank, who needed more than that? And he could always sell his stock, maybe even the house. He hated living there alone. Servants didn't count.

"Uh, Dad, I do have an heir."

"What?" The old man twisted suddenly in his seat, making the canoe lurch.

Rick was sure now the canoe was doing something more than drifting. He tried to see what the problem was. His father's fishing line was totally out of the water, riding taut a foot above the water's surface. He must be hooked on that log.

"Look at me, son. What do you mean, you have an heir?"

Rick had to focus back on his father. He took in a deep breath. "Remember Rosalind Karp?"

"That Jewess bitch at Ann Arbor?" The senior Tessel half-stood in the light canoe, waving his rod like a sword, yanking at the unyielding line.

"Yeah, Dad, when we were seniors at the University of Michigan. You didn't like her because you called her a beatnik and her father was a union organizer."

"I didn't like her because she was a kike! I made you see your ways, didn't I? What do you mean, an heir?"

"Yeah, you broke us up. You dragged me back to

9

Grosse Pointe and switched me to the University of Detroit and scared her within an inch of her life. But Rosalind was the love of my life, Dad."

"What about Susan?"

"Oh, Susan. Yes. I loved Susan, sort of. She was . . . almost like a best friend. I miss her. I still love Susan, in a way. But I'll always love Rosalind."

"The heir, stupid. What about the heir?"

His father's red face was an inch away. He felt dizzy — was it just his nerves from facing up to his father, or was his father rocking the canoe that badly?

He dug in with the paddle. His father yanked it from his hands. Rick grabbed it back and kept rowing. They were going in circles.

"Look at me — WHAT ABOUT THE HEIR?" It was a shout that reverberated along the walls of tall pines and painted rocks lining the river.

"She had a little girl and named her Tessela. Tessela Karp. Tessela Cutler now. She put me down on the birth certificate but didn't use Tessel as the kid's last name, just Tessela for the first name. Rosalind finally married a guy named Cutler and had a couple more kids, but I supported Tessela all these years. She's thirty-three now and lives in Los Angeles."

Tessel Senior struggled with the implications of the news. "Didn't Rosalind's husband adopt her? What does this . . . Tessela . . . do?" He spat out the bastardization of his name. "Is she married? Does she have children? More . . . heirs?"

"Uh, no, Dad. Rosalind never let her husband adopt her because she wanted Tessela to stay tied to our family. And she is. I put her through college,

University of Southern California, and then Antioch West for her master's. She's a therapist. And no, she's not married. No kids. No other heirs." He squirmed, wondering whether to drop the final bombshell.

"You've seen her? Why isn't she married? What's wrong with her? A woman that age should be married. She's not one of those bra burners, is she?"

"Say, Dad, hadn't we better see what's going on? The boat's floating pretty fast."

"To hell with the boat. Answer me, I can tell, you're keeping something from me, something else. TELL ME."

"Okay, all right, I'll tell you. She works for something like the Gay Service Center, something like that. She's not married because she's a lesbian."

"A kike dyke inheriting my money!" The old man sputtered and sat speechless. But only for a second. He roared: "Just wait till we get back, I'm going to change that will so fast your head's going to spin!"

"We are spinning, Dad." Paddle as hard as he might, Rick couldn't get the canoe back to the safety of the shallow, weedy shore. "What are you caught on, Dad? Let the rod go! We're being pulled into the current."

Tessel Senior tried to toss away his imported handcrafted fishing pole, but the line was now tangled around something in the bottom of the boat.

"Here, let me cut you free." Tessel Junior did a duckwalk along the canoe bottom toward his father, waving his Swiss Army knife. He lunged at the taut line and missed. The current grabbed hold and swung the canoe around broadside. Icy water sloshed over the side.

11

Sudden slack in the line made the boat spin anew in the racing current, more frothy white water splashing overboard.

A gigantic moose, its head and rack the size of a small sports car, reared out of the water and slashed at their canoe with its shaggy, dripping, monstrous hooves. For one second Rick imagined that it was the Superior Beer mascot arising from the rapids. A neon yellow and fluorescent green crawfish hung from one antler.

The punctured canoe spun and flew with the current, headed right for the first of the seven waterfalls that interrupted the river's rush to Lake Superior.

Only splinters made it to the lake.

The current pummeled Rick along the river's gravel bottom for such a long time that he finally had to attempt a breath and icy water poured into his lungs. He saw only a wall of pure red, his last thoughts of Rosalind and the life they should have had together.

Frederich Wilhelm Tessel's last thoughts were crazed with anger — at the moose, the river, his son, life in general, and in particular his unknown Jew dyke bastard granddaughter who had the nerve to be named Tessela and who was going to get all his hard-earned money.

CHAPTER ONE

"Laney, I'd like you to meet Tess Cutler. She wants to start another lesbian music festival someplace in Michigan. She's a therapist, used to work for the Gay and Lesbian Community Services Center. Tess, this is my assistant, Laney Samms, the one I was telling you about. By the way, Laney just got back from Michigan, too."

Kitt Meyers made the introductions perfunctorily as she bundled papers, files and computer supplies into boxes and disconnected the laser printer cable from her notebook Toshiba. Behind her, the fax machine birthed yet another document, which she managed to catch. She mumbled to herself as she read it, then tossed it in the overflowing trash. Kitt's favorite toy was that fax machine — she even used it instead of the phone to order pizza from across the street. All her friends and employees were on constant order to keep their fax lines open at all times. She liked it better than e-mail, preferring the immediate solidity of an emerging piece of paper to a transitory message that would take an extra second to print out.

I barely glanced at this Tess Cutler as we shook hands. Lucille Ball in a floral muu-muu, I thought to myself. The mention of Michigan had made my stomach hiccup and sink into my pelvis.

That's how low I felt, waiting for sixties rock star Hayley Malone to get her act together and decide, now that she was sober, if she wanted to be a closeted nineties rock star, a closeted member of her formerly estranged family, or an open lover of yours truly. Or all three simultaneously, if she wanted, just as long as that last item got in there somewhere.

Melissa Etheridge, k.d. lang and Janis Ian hadn't come out until they were firmly established, she'd kept pointing out when I tried to convince her the world didn't care anymore. Oh yes, it did, she assured me, and maybe she was right. And that was our last conversation in our on-hold relationship. If it was even on hold anymore.

I hadn't heard from her in a month, since she'd announced she had to stay with her brother and father back in Michigan rather than return to Los Angeles while she got her head together. She'd said she needed time. Without even a phone call, she'd already sent me a message, but I still thought I should wait some more. Her trip to Michigan had been frightfully traumatic, and you couldn't expect someone to assimilate all the family information she'd recently learned so quickly. But not even a call?

I was wondering seriously whether we'd ever really had a relationship.

Had I just succumbed to serial lust again, the way I'd done until I was twenty-eight, before Anne rescued me and put me back together for the next twenty years? At the thought of the way I'd messed up with Anne, I felt even worse. This downward spiral had to stop, and quickly.

I forced myself to look Tess Cutler in the eyes. They were laughing green, happily flecked with gold and circled with brown. Carrot red hair in a short spiky halo. A wide smile. Round dimpled cheeks, very little neck, short round body. A flowery long-waisted loose jumper over a yellow T-shirt. Worn black ballerina flats. Bare, pale, solid legs, shaven. A sense she was her own woman, to hell with fashion, she liked the way she looked. Comfortable, to be sure.

And what a smile! Perfectly formed tiny white teeth, lips in a perfect bow shape as if drawn on with lip liner. Betty Boop lips. The look was an inch short of floozy, a half inch short of sloppy, and well over the line of friendly. Bette Midler flooze. Not my type, but someone I liked instinctively.

I grinned back. Gee, I almost felt good in spite of myself. She was probably a great therapist. She'd cheer up her patients just by smiling at them.

"Laney, could you bring the Viper around back? I've got so much to drag home, I don't want to make two trips down the back stairs. Take those files on your way down." Kitt nodded toward a stack of manila folders. "You'll have to take Tess's suitcase back to the house in your Jeep."

My look asked the question.

"Yes, she'll be staying with me a few days. You won't believe the *chutzpa* of this woman. All week long on the phone I've been telling her I can't handle the job she wants me to do, so she flies in to LAX and demands I come get her, we have to talk in person. I should have left her sitting at the terminal. She never heard of cabs?"

I had to check Kitt's face to make sure she was joking. This Tess was beaming like a cat with a feather on its lips.

"But no, the nerve of this woman, I can't believe it, so I drop everything to go get her! Just to see for myself what kind of person would do such a thing." She motioned at the mammoth soft-side green paisley suitcase in the corner. "And she brings along her entire wardrobe to boot. I had to tie it in the trunk and drive with the lid open. We must have made quite a sight, squeezed into the Viper."

Kitt has that same kind of almost but not quite put-together look, but she spends thousands of dollars each year trying to keep it that way. I can't help comparing Kitt to an English sheep dog, and her gray-streaked black shag always looks as if she desperately needs a haircut so that she can peer out from under the long bangs, even when she's just spent eighty dollars with Ermando at Jon Peters salon. Her T-shirt cost a hundred and seventy thousand lira in Rome; mine was one of Kitt's unsold leftovers from an early Indigo Girls tour. A perk of my job — all the women's music T-shirts I want. So I live in them, over jeans or cutoffs.

Kitt drives a flame red Dodge Viper two-seater V-12 sports car, insured for every penny of its $70,000 price tag, and worries every time she brings it to her West Hollywood office on Santa Monica Boulevard. There's usually an open parking space in the alley beside an abandoned building around the corner and across the side street from Kitt's office building. We can see the car from one of her office windows, a selling point for that spot.

From a few feet away I took Kitt's key ring out of my jeans pocket and made the Viper's alarm system chirp off. Something moving on the ground caught my eye. Probably a rat. The palm trees near the office were full of them, as was the shin-deep, ground cover ivy that survives anywhere in L.A. that grass can't. You think the wind's making the ivy rustle, until you realize there's no wind. I love L.A.

But it was a longhaired kitten that crawled out from under a dumpster near the Viper, and I detoured to pet the tiny tabby. She — of course a kitten was a she, until proven otherwise — arched her back and fluffed her tail for me, circling my Reeboks and rubbing my ankles.

"Aren't you a cutie!" I cooed like a fool, glancing quickly around me. Don't let anybody see this old butch babytalking to a cat.

Up close I could see she had four white feet, a heart-shaped white patch under her chin, and a white lightning slash on her nose, the mark of Zorro. Her back markings were mostly the traditional brown, black and tan ticking of a tabby, except for some

17

orange patches that looked sponged on, like someone had tried to make a calico out of the mundane tabbiness. Her puffed tail was striped like a raccoon, only in orange, tabby and white. A decidedly unusual kitten.

At first I automatically named her Zorro, then decided that was a male name, and she was probably a female because of the calico touch to her markings. She arched her back and glanced over her shoulder at me. Her white whiskers twitched. "You little flirt," I said aloud. Flirt, that was her name.

Her backbone was sharp to my fingers. She tried desperately to nurse from my fingertips. Her skin had no resiliency under the fluff; she was severely dehydrated. L.A. hadn't had rain in ages. How much longer could she last in this alley? I had to save this kitten, but when I grabbed for her, she dashed back under the dumpster.

I stood up, hands on my hips. "Okay, Flirt, if you want to live, you have to come out. You don't want to die under a dumpster. Not in one, either. Haul your tail out here and let me take you home." I heard her crying but saw nothing.

When I got on my knees, she darted farther back, out of reach, but teased me by coming forward when I got up again. We repeated this dance a few times until I gave up. I can't save every animal in the world, though Anne seemed to think it was possible. She's a veterinarian, the best. She'd pull this kitten through, no matter how sick it was. The cat stayed out of reach.

It was a painful thought, but maybe I wasn't going to be able to rescue Flirt. Maybe it wasn't meant to be. Kitt probably wouldn't have wanted another cat around her place since she's got a houseful of purebred Maine Coons and Scottish Folds.

Maybe it was best that the kitten just disappeared from view and I never thought of it again. Though I knew the image of that little baby kitten flirting with me would ruin the rest of my day if I didn't save her. Sadly, I gave up and stretched my six-foot frame out straight. There was that annoying twinge in my right hip again. I'm too old to be crawling under dumpsters, I told myself.

Suddenly there was Flirt again, teasing me. I lunged for her. She raced back under the dumpster. This time the garbage smell caught me full in the lungs and made me choke.

I cursed and got into the red convertible and waited, keeping my eyes straight ahead so she wouldn't think I was watching for her.

After a long moment I gave up and turned the key. The motor purred to life. At the same instant she crawled out from under the dumpster again. I leaped out of the car and pounced. "Gotcha!"

The momentum and my sideways dive carried me to the other side of the dumpster, where I got my hands firmly around the kitten and clutched her to my chest. She was all claws, slashing away at my face and arms. My left foot hung out in the alley, hurting from the way I'd slid.

The Viper exploded.

Steel sliced the sole of my left foot right through my Reebok. The rest of me, protected by the dumpster, felt a wave of heat and flame blow overhead, singeing my hair. A rain of flaming embers set fire to my T-shirt in a dozen places; I rolled to put out the fire, holding on to the cat through it all.

19

With one hand I slapped out an ash burning on top of my scalp. I checked the cat. My body had protected her. She was still flailing away, trying to escape, crying pitifully, terrified.

All around me were strewn hunks of sizzling-hot metal, chunks of blackened leather seatcovers, molten glass. Heavy black smoke rolled from what was left of the tires. Melt-down.

"Laney!" I heard a scream from far away.

In a few seconds Kitt and Tess were at my side, helping me to my feet. Tess tried to take the cat. "Watch it, she's a wiry little devil," I said.

Tess finally used the hem of her jumper like an apron to wrap around Flirt's claws and immobilize the scrawny kitten, while Kitt brushed off debris and checked me out. Once she saw I was all right, she began stomping her feet and flailing her arms at the skies. "My new car! I love that car!"

A siren sounded in the distance. We stomped on the first flames spreading to the patches of grass in the gravel alleyway. Flames roared from a chunk of upholstery atop the dumpster.

The first fire truck to arrive blew billowing white foam all over the Viper's carcass to squelch gasoline fires. A police officer was right behind the fire fighters, moving us away from the wreck, back down the alley and into the street.

We answered the officer's questions and tried to figure out what had happened. Other police cars arrived and officers swarmed over the wreckage. Shaking, I took Flirt from Tess and hugged her close to me and found myself fighting tears. She'd saved my life.

CHAPTER TWO

After checking once more that I was all right,
Kitt stared at the molten heap of ashes and twisted
metal, all the while moaning and groaning and
rubbing her shaggy-thatched head. She walked around
the remnants, kicking what seemed to be a piece of
CD player with her Birkenstocks.

"God, I'll miss that car," she said. "People look at
you so differently when you're behind the wheel of a
red sports car. Zero to sixty in four and a half
seconds."

"That last trip it went even faster, straight up," I said. "Sorry," I added when she glared at me.

I was going to miss it too, though I wouldn't trade my new sky-blue Jeep Cherokee four-by-four Sport for it. Kitt never had any room for anything, so I always had to come bail her out. She'd had a cellular phone installed in mine specifically so that she could call me anywhere when she needed me — or rather, my spacious car.

The Viper's price had included a couple thousand dollars extra for gas guzzler tax, which it soundly deserved. And who needs a car that has to be guarded every second? I'd always worried about being carjacked when I took it on errands for Kitt. Not that any car is immune.

I had my burns bandaged and my foot wound cleaned out at an emergency clinic on Sunset while Tess and Kitt ate at Burrito King. They brought me back a quesadilla and horchata.

The cut required six stitches and an updated tetanus shot. I'd have to tiptoe and hop for a while and change the bandage three times a day. I promised to come back in a week to have the stitches removed. Sure. I'd snip and pull them myself, if there was no infection.

Kitt did the driving back to Mount Washington in my Jeep. "Hey, handles good. How's your mileage? I've got to go through all the hassle of getting another car now. Maybe I'll lease a couple models before I buy. Maybe something inconspicuous. Another Beemer. Or a Lexus. Blend in with the crowd." The right crowd.

Kitt's questions about the Jeep took my mind off my foot and off my narrow escape. After the fact, my life was passing before my eyes. All the chances I didn't take. All the years I wasted. I patted the kitten, who was still wrapped up in Tess's jumper, meowing and purring simultaneously.

"Say, do you think Anne would take care of your kitten?" Kitt finally asked, when she'd exhausted her line of inquiry about Cherokees. "She's probably got fleas and worms and who knows what all else. Anne will get her fixed up."

We left it hanging on what would happen after that. So Kitt's a bit of a snob. But the cat would be in the guest house, nowhere near her purebreds. If Kitt agreed, I'd let her run loose, catch some of the baby rats and mice in the ivy. Or if Kitt insisted, she could be an indoor cat. Probably safer that way. Too many coyotes roam Mount Washington. I'd have to figure out something so she didn't escape out Radar's doggie door.

"Do you want me to drive over to Anne's clinic now?" Kitt interrupted my thoughts.

I gulped. I hadn't seen Anne in months. It felt like decades. "Yeah, I guess so." I glanced at my watch. "She might even be home already."

Kitt and her toys — she used the cellular phone to dial the clinic first, then asked me for directions to Anne's house. My old house.

I guided Kitt through the winding roads of Silverlake to the two-bedroom porched stucco cottage — lost in the gold hillside chaparral, overlooking the teal-green Silverlake reservoir — that Anne and I had shared for nearly twenty years.

My stomach churned. It was the first time I'd been back since Anne finally ordered me out. With good reason. Some two years ago I'd decided that I was suffering from midlife crisis and needed to find myself, after having let myself slip into a life that was pretty much determined by Anne.

I'd realized that I was living her life, not my own. I'd become just a prematurely silver-haired tall dyke who looked good in a tux, escorting Anne to all the formal benefits sponsored by the community organizations which had both of us on their boards of directors. We'd drifted to the point where more than a year had gone by without sex. Without a meaningful conversation. It happens.

I could see now that in part, it wasn't even a lesbian thing. It was the eternal underlying battle between the secure comfort of commitment with its sometimes monotonous monogamy, and the uncertain danger of the search for perpetual, all-consuming passion. Easy to say now, but not when your head's whirling. Millions of men and women, gay and straight, make the wrong choice.

After Anne and I broke up, a married woman came after me like a sledge hammer and really did a number on my head. But all the while I'd still lived in Anne's house, occupying the second bedroom formerly reserved for her grown son's visits on semester breaks from Stanford. Finally Anne had had enough.

When the lawyers were through separating twenty years of financial entanglements, Anne kept the house and I kept Samms', the Silverlake bar which she'd bought for me in 1972 but which I'd made into a success. Enough so that I could leave it in the hands of my manager most of the time. Sometimes I felt guilty cashing the profit checks. But while I'd been content to run a watering hole for dinosaurs, Carmen brought to the bar a younger, hipper image, able to compete with Girl Bar, with dueling sexy ads in the L.A. *Lesbian News.*

Sometimes one of my old customers called to complain. As my friend Max put it, "Where do old butches go for a drink these days?" Beats me. As a recovering alcoholic, I'd been able to handle the presence of booze for years, but over the last few years it seemed better to stay away from the joint, except for occasional special events.

Kitt had hired me as a glorified house-sitter for her Mount Washington hilltop estate, and gradually I'd gotten more and more involved in her multi-faceted company, Meyers Music. From there I'd gotten more and more involved with Hayley Malone. But Anne and I had somehow remained friends. And now I was going to impose on her once more. She didn't owe me any favors, but I knew she'd take Flirt anyway, for as long as it took to nurse her back to health. Permanently, if need be, if I couldn't convince Kitt that Flirt wouldn't somehow contaminate her purebreds. Check *pushover* in the dictionary.

Anne was on the porch swing, two cats on her lap, four lapdogs attempting to surreptitiously nuzzle the felines off. Like shaggy caterpillars late for dinner, the Shih Tzu and Pomeranian came running and yapping as we pulled into her drive.

"Hi! What on earth happened to you!" Anne dropped both cats and ran to open the gate to the chain-link fence for the Jeep. Like a soccer player, she used her feet to keep the dogs inside. I noticed she was still in her hospital-green scrubs. It apparently hadn't been a hard day at the office or she would have ditched them immediately.

Her short, curvy figure was as agile as ever as she fought back the animals. One thing I'd learned from Anne was that menopause was not the end of the world. Maybe that fear had spurred my disastrous behavior that horrible year. I'd laughed at the concept of midlife crisis, but how else to explain my stupidity? My periods were becoming, I had to admit, a wee bit irregular, my skin a little drier. Could hot flashes be far behind? Anne had always made jokes about hers, but I didn't look forward to my own fireworks.

I made the introductions and briefly told Anne what had happened.

"That's horrible! You poor thing! Let me take a look at that foot."

So she wasn't bearing me any hard feelings today. Her professional touch felt cool and strong. I sniffed; her signature perfume was still flea dip. I had to grin, it all felt so familiar. She didn't notice.

"Okay, you'll live," she pronounced judgment on the clinic's work, finally giving me a rare smile. She asked to see my prescription for antibiotics and nodded as she read.

Her royal blue eyeglass frames always made her eyes look deeper in color. She'd let her curly salt-and-pepper hair grow shoulder-length again. For some reason the tousled waves made me think of an undyed Barbara Walters getting out of bed. It felt very, very good to have Anne showing concern for me. I smiled back and tried to keep her gaze focused in my direction. She met my eyes.

Instantly she reverted to cool reserve toward me, though she was her usual friendly self toward Tess and Kitt. Tess introduced her to the kitten, who had finally fallen asleep on her lap. The kitten awoke and yawned in Anne's face and the vet was in love: "What a pink nose! What precious little white whiskers! What a thick coat on such a tiny baby! But she's so thin! Don't worry, kitty, we'll get you fattened up in no time!"

She told me to pour four cold drinks while she took Flirt into the bathroom. No more of my Diet Pepsis in her fridge, only Anne's preferred Vernor's, so I made four iced teas. Tess helped hold down the kitten while Anne used gauze and warm water to clean off the furry face.

"We won't use the flea shampoo on you yet, babycat, but it's coming, yes it is," I heard Anne's assurances. "We'll get those bad parasites with a flea comb so they won't hurt you anymore."

If only some of the gay male board of director members Anne terrorized into giving more money to some cause or another could see her with an animal in trouble!

Kitt stayed in the living room and kept Anne's menagerie entertained. I could hear her repeatedly shooing assorted animals off of her lap.

"You are such a sweetie-pie!" Anne kept cooing to the kitten when she brought it back out.

I'd known it would be love at first sight.

She squeezed a dollop of Nutra-Cal food supplement from a tube onto her finger and let Flirt suckle. "You're going to be fine, just fine," she assured the feline.

We chatted for a while, then left. I was

overwhelmingly exhausted, though it had to be psychological.

"Your mind is the hardest-working muscle of all," Tess said when we were back in the car and I'd sagged across the rear seat of my Cherokee.

"I think that's the heart," I said. So Tess's anatomy was a little off; her intentions were good. She flashed that well-shaped smile and I felt better. I'd survived another encounter with Anne, and she'd been downright pleasant. Even concerned about me. Too bad I'd thrown the baby out with the bathwater.

Oh well, it was too late now. Anne had made that painfully clear two years ago. "I could never take you back," she'd said. "It really is over." Her exact words. And she'd meant it.

My Higher Power kicked me in the tail and brought me back to the present.

Mainly I was relieved that Anne had taken Flirt. I felt forever linked to the kitten that had saved my life. As I had hers.

And now I had another ongoing link with Anne. Somehow in the lesbian community you're never totally free from old lovers. In the bad old days I'd walked into some parties and walked right out again at the sight of too many, too familiar, faces.

Now it's as if there isn't any more lesbian community, none that I feel a part of anyway; all of us dinosaurs are off living our own lives and letting the ACT UP crowd and the lipstick lesbians do their thing. I see a long-ago lover across the crowd at a concert and it's a relief — we still exist. We lived. And we're not dead yet. I've got a few kicks left in me, as I'd found out with Hayley.

28

* * * * *

The next morning a raucous ringing woke me in the guest house. A Detective Clyde Jefferson from the bomb squad was on the phone, saying he needed more information. He was on his way. I stretched and my whole body ached. The stitches on my left foot itched and smarted.

The thought of another policeman on the property brought back memories. Last summer Kitt and I had called the cops to stop a rape we saw going on in the alley, next to where her Viper had been parked. We didn't realize that the men moving equipment into the abandoned building were setting up a drug lab — until they'd reacted to the sight of the cops by drawing their artillery.

Five men ended up going to jail as a result, and it had been Kitt's name on the nine-one-one report that had called the cops to the site. It was her unmistakable Viper on the scene. Ergo, she must have been the target of the explosion. That's what we told the cops. Except they disagreed.

"It was your standard car bomb," Detective Jefferson said. "Gunpowder, pipe, blasting pin, fuse set off by the car's ignition spark, and detonator cord. But pretty professional." He was slightly built and must have gotten onto the force when the height requirements were eased to reflect L.A.'s changing population. He stroked his pockmarked copper face as if his morning shave had hurt. It probably had.

"How come I got away?" I asked.

"The guy left a few seconds' length on the detonator cord, probably to make sure the car's occupants were really settled in. If he'd wanted, he could have made it go off when you were down the block or home again."

He said that bomb experts often deliberately leave little I.D. tags in their work — their peculiar kind of wire, or a special kind of pipe or tape, or a certain way of winding the wire. Pride of workmanship, I guess.

"This one's giveaway is a particular kind of imported blasting pin he gets from a Toronto hobby store," Detective Jefferson said. "He has no ties to your friends in jail. They're chumps, rank amateurs, not in this guy's league. They couldn't afford him. They got caught over a really stupid mistake, and this guy's been eluding us for years. He's a slam-dunk kind of guy — breezes into town, makes a hit and disappears into another city." His words were chilling. And it got worse. "I know you think this bombing has to be tied to that earlier incident, but we're talking about something entirely different here. Laney probably wasn't the real target, but it could have been Tess as well as Kitt. Or both of you."

The two of them exchanged frightened glances.

Jefferson nodded in their direction. "Sounds like the two of you were none too subtle driving in from the airport, and you could have been followed. Maybe the longer time on the fuse was to allow both Tess and Kitt to get into the car again. Tess, think about who knew you were coming to L.A. and when. Kitt, make a list of your enemies. Don't worry, we'll check it out."

Don't worry, be happy. They wrote down every name they could think of for the police. Kitt would write down a name, shake her head, erase it, and then write it again. Tess simply looked puzzled. Jefferson left with their lists. He called several times to say nothing was panning out and to press for any more details they could remember.

Detectives recommended even tighter security measures at Kitt's Mount Washington estate and at her office. She hired round-the-clock security guards again, as we'd had for part of the summer with our celebrity houseguest Hayley Malone. Originally Kitt had asked me to live in the guest house as a kind of glorified house sitter, when she'd heard I was looking for a new place to live after Anne and I broke up. Next I was elevated to baby sitter for Hayley Malone when she finished her fourth stay at the Betty Ford Center. Gradually Kitt kept finding more and more uses for my varied talents, and she kept hiking my salary, but I've never had a real title or clear-cut duties. Somewhere along the way I understood I was no longer the house sitter. The security guards making the rounds at deliberately erratic hours made that job unnecessary.

As a few days passed, we learned to live with their presence. Kitt and Tess spent a lot of time together, and I kept overhearing snippets of conversation that indicated Kitt was saying no a lot. Unlike me, she has no trouble with that word.

After high school in Detroit, I went into the Army instead of to college and got stuck typing news releases in the public relations office. After getting caught in a lavender purge, my dishonorable discharge — and my drinking — doomed me to a series of menial jobs. I met Anne when I was grooming dogs, and she saw something in this silver head that caught her attention and led to my salvation.

Through the years I've taken all the courses in the UCLA Extension Public Relations Program, plus additional classes in desktop publishing, advertising and marketing, so Kitt plugs me into all sorts of roles at Meyers Music. Usually she sticks me with the dirty jobs she'd rather not do herself.

And since the explosion and Tess's badgering, I could tell from the way I sometimes caught her looking at me across the room and averting her eyes that she had something in mind, something I wasn't going to like. I practiced mouthing the word, "No."

CHAPTER THREE

"Laney, we've been through a lot of stress here lately. How'd you like to get out of town until this thing blows over? A little change of scenery."

Kitt was pretending to be nonchalant, sipping the last of her lemonade after dinner, looking with great interest at the squeezed lemon half inside her Waterford glass. I could see her eyes shift just enough to take in my reaction.

I stared at her. What else was on her mind? Okay, I'd play along. "Tahiti? You're sending me to Tahiti? I'll go pack right now." I'd seen a travel brochure on the island and it kept popping up in my mind.

She laughed. "I had in mind asking you to go back to Michigan with Tess for the next couple of weeks and help her set up this music festival thing. You've seen me work, you know the kinds of things that have to be taken care of."

Kitt got up and began putting away the remnants of our stir fry dinner. Nothing out of the ordinary, her behavior said. A slight rigidity to her posture gave her away. One of the problems of living so close to your boss is that you become friends, and then the boss-employee line can become unclear. Sometimes it has to be redrawn.

I don't completely disagree with lesbian feminists who keep wanting to make employees and bosses equal peers, aiming for consensus, rather than blunt orders. Still, some jobs never get done by mere suggestions and hints. So we were having one of those touchy moments.

I had a million objections, all of which I knew would be fruitless, starting with, "Why don't you go?"

"I can't get away. I've got two clients wanting to jump ship now that their careers are taking off, right at the moment when all my hard work getting them launched will start to pay off. Nobody has any gratitude anymore. I told Tess I had to stay here to keep on top of that situation, plus I don't want to leave the house right now. In fact I kept turning Tess down by phone when she was in Michigan, which is why she showed up in L.A. to convince me otherwise. I did say I could spare someone on my staff, and I'd supervise. She says she has confidence you can do the job."

"I've never done this kind of work before."

"You set up your bar and made it a successful business, enough that you could turn it over to a manager and just rake in profits. You started a public relations business — yes, I know it's small, but your customers love you. You pulled off a quickie ad campaign for that concert I got together at the last minute. And you handled Hayley's problems all right. Don't underestimate yourself."

It must have been obvious that I wasn't convinced. But she was skilled enough to see that I wasn't totally adverse to the idea either, and we both knew why.

"Look, I'll make a checklist, and I'll come out to see the place in a couple of weeks. Your main job will be to get some experts in there to do the job right, and to keep her focused. Tess makes it sound as if everything she's tried has gone wrong, and she's blowing a ton of money. She's apparently got plenty from an inheritance, but still, no sense in wasting it."

Kitt grew up with money and has a fine eye for budget line items. I've learned from her, but Anne always handled the money in our relationship. I told Kitt so.

"I know, but you'll do fine. You know more than you think. From what Tess says, you need to get out there right away to look at the grounds. You need to get a good look at the layout, see what the entire facility can handle, before the whole place gets buried in a snowbank. They get a *lot* of snow, she tells me. It's someplace up north, out in the boonies. A skiing area."

"Around Traverse City?" That was the most popular resort area in Michigan that I could recall.

"Umm, there's the phone. I guess, if that's where they have skiing. Just a second."

"What exactly do you want done?" I asked when she came back into the kitchen.

"Oh, see if the place needs an overhaul by an interior decorator, get good people in from the beginning on designing the stage, get the best lighting and sound people committed, come up with some marketing ideas, make it something different from the Michigan Womyn's Music Festival, check out the community for potential problems, see if there's any great local talent, size up the media . . . you know the routine."

I was glad she thought so.

"Once you get some dates set I'll round up the acts. Get a business plan out of her, and a budget. You may need to find a local accountant and lawyer to cross all the *t*s. I'll have Adrienne put everything you need on disks, and you can reach me by e-mail or phone anytime. I'll fax you anything else you need." She brushed aside my continued objections. "Do what you can and I'll fly out in a few weeks to wrap things up. We'll be back here before Christmas. Nobody gets any work done around Christmas anyway."

"Is that enough time?"

"I don't know if we can pull off a music festival this fast, but we'll see. No harm in starting small — but not too small. She really wants something to happen next summer, though I suspect that's too soon. See if you can bring it off, and if it's not possible, smooth her feelings and make it work for next year."

I was not thrilled with being the one who might have to tell Tess her expectations were too high. It sounded as if she thought Meyers Music was going to be able to work wonders. And I was supposed to be Wonder Woman.

"Fly out with her and rent a four-by-four for the snow," Kitt continued. "Hey, see if you can lease a Jeep Cherokee like your own since you love it so much. In fact, I may buy a Grand Cherokee myself this time, something practical for a change. Though I saw a Ferrari I liked the other day." Her mind wandered just for a second, I could tell by watching her eyes. Then she was back on track, out to get me on her track.

I had no fond memories of snow and couldn't remember how to drive in the stuff. I doubted it was like riding a bicycle. I glared at Kitt. She stood her ground.

"Laney, this lady needs help. She spent most of the summer throwing money around at this hunting lodge thing she inherited, and she needs some control. It sounds like a gigantic money pit. I'll give you a new title — hey, we never did have one for you. Consider this a promotion to, what . . . how about Events Coordinator? With an appropriate increase in pay, and I know Tess is generous with expenses. How about it?"

She was almost being flirtatious, cocking her head to the side and giving me a teasing smile. The money was more seductive than her familiar ploys. I was trying to stockpile my retirement fund, after skimping on it for too many years. When you're young and the savings could really mount up, you think you'll never get old.

Kitt sure could pour it on — everything but the eyelashes were in action, and I thought maybe I detected a flutter even there. Despite living together, with only a pool separating the two houses, we'd never been attracted to each other physically. Both too butch to bend. Her attempt at flirting, even more than the raise, was an indication of her desperation. She wanted me to go, but she didn't like to draw that line. She didn't want to give me that blunt order, but it was still an assignment. If I said no, it could mean my job. And I was the logical person. Plus the other factor.

"Michigan," I said, unable to summon any positive emotion at returning to my home state, though I was pleased with the promotion, now that it was couched in those terms. I'd left Michigan at age eighteen to join the Army and would have never gone back if it hadn't been for Hayley's necessary trip in October. "Long way from Tahiti."

"Yes, Michigan." She paused.

I waited.

She broke first. "Yes, I know Hayley's in Michigan. Isn't she staying someplace near Detroit?"

"Rochester," I reminded her. "It's a nice suburb. At her brother's."

"So maybe I do have a hidden agenda. It won't hurt to have you within shouting distance while Hayley makes her decision. Who knows, she might decide to let me be her agent after all, when she gets out of this slump."

She nudged me with her elbow, still putting on the flirtatious act. She saw that I saw, and stopped.

"And maybe it'll get you out of your slump, too — *three* birds with one stone. Hey, I'll throw in hazard pay for the snow. Tess is offering big bucks, and I'm passing most of it on to you. If and when she gets this music festival thing going, it will be a great opportunity for me. Good competition for the Michigan Womyn's Music Festival, but it has to be different somehow. This thing could be really big. I want this contract. Come on, it's a challenge."

I have to admit, I enjoy watching my boss beg.

"How much extra pay?"

We haggled. I gave in, gracefully but not cheaply.

So Tess and I made arrangements to fly back. She wanted to stop in Detroit to talk with the Tessel lawyers, and the only place I could find a Jeep Cherokee available to rent was at Metro anyway. Since it was a direct flight on Northwest, I decided to bring Radar along. She'd be company out in the wilds. Ever since I almost lost her to drowning last summer, I've wanted her close.

I talked to my AA sponsor, Mara Wilgrein, who reminded me to pack my AA literature and said I should at least try an occasional meeting in Michigan. I feared that my being a dyke from L.A. would get in the way of being heard by the stereotypical backwoods drunks I imagined; Mara said to trust in the process, and in my Higher Power, who had been awfully quiet when I made this decision.

I had to find new AA sponsors for the two

newcomers I'd taken on recently, and I also had to make some arrangements with other board members of AIDS Aid to fulfill some of my commitments that I'd be missing. Carmen assured me everything was going fine at Samms', and I checked with the small Silverlake stores for which I do PR, to make sure they wouldn't need me the next couple of weeks. I brought one of Kitt's assistants along with me and told the store owners she would be their contact while I was gone — clients like to have a face to go with the name and number you're leaving in your place. Not a whole lot to have to do to leave a life behind.

I'd packed my ski things and the few thick sweaters and sweats I had, but Tess promised to get me outfitted right when we arrived. Long thermal underwear, for instance. I itched just thinking about it.

"They tell me the last eight or ten winters have been mild," she assured me. "It keeps getting warmer — everybody says it's the greenhouse effect. It won't be that bad."

Uh huh. "How cold was it when you left?"

"Oh, we'd had a few inches of snow already. But it melted. I checked the Weather Channel — it's not socked in yet. It will be, but hopefully we'll be out of there soon."

"You had no problems adjusting to snow even though you'd been living in L.A. before that?"

"I didn't say that." Tess made a coughing sound. "But I like winter sports, especially snow mobiling. I've been thinking about the possibility of spending the whole winter there, or at least staying a little longer after you leave. I keep toying with the idea of

doing something with the lodge year-round, though I
don't know what. A lesbian ski lodge perhaps? Maybe
you'll come up with some ideas. There's not much
anybody *can* do during the worst of the winter except
ski."

Great.

We had a smooth flight, and Radar made the trip
in good spirits. I couldn't help worrying about her
after the recent news reports about accidents to
animals on airlines, though the statistics are no
worse than those for people having mishaps on
planes. The waiting Cherokee was black and gold,
and per Kitt's instructions it had a cellular phone
already installed. I called her from Metro to tell her
we'd arrived safely. There were no last-minute
instructions.

Tess bought an atlas at the airport to find the
quickest route into Grosse Pointe Park to see the
Tessel lawyers, and then to the lodge. We agreed: I'd
drive, she'd navigate. Detroit Metro is right on the
I-94, which goes very close to Grosse Pointe as it
winds its way northeast, and from there we'd find
I-75 to take us due north.

"My grandfather's lodge is in the Upper
Peninsula, almost to the border of Wisconsin," she
said, studying the Rand McNally. "It's near a little
town called Beer Barrel, I guess because of my
grandfather's business. It's too small to be on the
map. Population three hundred and seventy-two, but
who's counting?"

She looked over to see if I was laughing. I wasn't.
In fact, I was in shock. When Kitt had said
someplace up north, I'd imagined Traverse City or
maybe nearby Grayling, one of the resort regions in

the Lower Peninsula. Did Kitt even know how big Michigan was? She could be excused — she's not great on Midwest geography. But had Tess deliberately kept the exact location from me? What else hadn't she told me?

"The closest big town is Ironwood, which has around seven thousand. Double that in the outlying area."

"Big."

"Hey, Ironwood even has a Kmart. It'll seem like L.A. after you see Beer Barrel."

Beer Barrel. I remembered the town of Bad Axe in the Michigan Thumb. And Ubly and Argyle and Elmer and Pigeon and Pinnebog and Lum and a dozen other crazy names. Are the people who choose the names for small towns all nuts? My favorite Michigan small town is named Hell, and it regularly freezes over.

"Ironwood's only a hundred miles from Duluth and nearly six hundred from Detroit," Tess went on.

Why hadn't I pinned down Tess on the exact location of this lodge before I signed up? I grabbed the atlas from her and kept glancing at it as I drove. The Upper Peninsula was indeed a long, long way from where I'd grown up in and around Detroit in the southeast part of the state, and it looked even farther away on the map. I'd lived in L.A. too long to remember the Upper Peninsula in any detail. Incredibly vivid fall colors was my predominant impression.

Vaguely I remembered a doomed vacation with my father and one of his three wives after my mother left. The trip had started with a day-long wait for the ferry to the Upper Peninsula, before the five-mile-long Mackinac Bridge was built connecting the state's two halves. While he'd pitched a tent for us on the shores of a place aptly called Mosquito Lake, the wife and I, in a rare show of unity, had pitched a fit. I was sent to some aunt's house to live when we got home. That wife hadn't lasted much longer.

"So how do you expect to draw people to the middle of nowhere for a music festival?" I asked.

"Ironwood's not the boonies, it's a booming ski region. You sound like Kitt — she thinks the world ends at the L.A. County line except for a little patch of inferior civilization on Manhattan. My grandfather's lodge is within five hundred miles of Minneapolis, Milwaukee, Chicago, Des Moines, Fargo, even Winnipeg. Plenty of underserved lesbians in the Midwest."

Maybe. At least she'd thought that part out. "I guess it'll be good competition for the Michigan Womyn's Music Festival. It should attract a different crowd and maybe draw off some of their attendees too," I mused aloud. MWMF was at Hart each August, on the west side of the mitten-shaped lower peninsula, which made it almost as far from Beer Barrel as Detroit was.

"We'll see. I don't want to get that big," Tess said. "They bring in seven thousand women! Some women in Duluth just started a small-scale weekend festival called Northern Lights, using local talent. That's too small for what I have in mind. I'm thinking more along the lines of a resort holiday festival, not wilderness camping. Though I'd like a camping area for those who can't afford to rent the cabins and lodge."

"Kitt told me. The resort concept is your biggest selling point. Not everyone likes to rough it. We both think you should aim for July when it's the most beautiful and your festival gets the jump start. It sounds good," I said, thinking some more. "I just hope we have enough time to pull this thing off."

And then it hit me — I was going to be more out of reach of Hayley in the Upper Peninsula than I would be in L.A. It was like moving to San Diego in hopes of meeting Holly Near on the beach.

Oh well, Hayley hadn't called anyway. A phone could be silent in the Upper Peninsula as easily as in L.A.

CHAPTER FOUR

Driving through downtown Detroit was a wrenching experience. Even from the pot-holed freeway, the shells of hundreds of abandoned, charred buildings were clearly visible. For years the city leadership has poured most of its resources into making the riverfront beautiful again, and it is. To hell with the neighborhoods. The new mayor promises things will be different. I hope so. I cringed as I drove through what felt like a war zone. The city and suburbs seemed even more clearly segregated than they were when I was a child.

And then there was Grosse Pointe Shores, a genteel residential community like a transported Bel Air, minus red Spanish tile roofs and bougainvillea. Red brick and snow slush instead. Tess showed me the two mansions she'd briefly owned in the inheritance and which were now being remodeled by their new owners. The lawyers were on Moross in Grosse Pointe Park, where most Pointe businesses were located.

After Tess signed some papers we took I-75 north. My stomach wrenched as we went by the exit that led toward Rochester and Hayley's brother's home.

Tess told me the story of how her mother and father met at U of M and fell in love, only to be broken apart by the man who was behind Superior Beer. It was bottled near Sault Ste. Marie, from pure Lake Superior waters, the ads bragged. They featured a huge bull moose, the Superior Beer mascot. In recent years the bull began to wear shades, like Joe Camel, in an attempt to win the younger macho customer base.

"Apparently my father never told his dad about me, and I inherited the fortune kind of accidentally," she said, green eyes twinkling. "The lawyers fought over the will for years."

"So you're in charge of Superior Beer?"

"Oh sure. What do I know about hops? I'm still the majority stockholder, but I told the accountants to figure out how I can get rid of the company. Tessel had two other children besides my dad. One's a nun, but the other's a queen in Key West who's making noises about buying me out, which would be great. He needs to get some capital, though. His father didn't leave him anywhere near what I got."

I glanced over at her. She shrugged. "I told you I got the money kind of accidentally. It's not like he's hurting — he's a millionaire already. Anyway, there's a rumor that one of the other beer companies is interested in buying a majority stock interest, which is okay too. You know how the trend now is toward small gourmet beer labels, even though they're owned by the same big companies that keep the masses stupefied. I don't want to have anything to do with Tessel Corporation except to spend the money."

Sitting on this woman's spending habits might be hard.

"Apparently there's a Tessel Foundation which runs a couple other businesses and gives money to charities. The lawyers earned their chunk trying to figure out where the foundation ended and my share began. That's why I had to stop by their offices and sign more papers."

A groan came from the back seat. Radar needed a walk. No rest stop coming for miles. I pulled over to the side of the freeway and snapped on her chain leash while she danced in anticipation. Tess stretched her legs and continued to talk while I let Radar find the exact weed that needed watering.

"Once I got the money, right off the bat I took an extended leave of absence from GLCSC and flew out to see the place. One look at the lodge and I knew it would make a great lesbian resort. It'll serve Tessel right. *If* I can get this music festival off the ground."

I gave her the proper reassurance as we got back on the road.

"Finally it hit me that I'd never have to work again, so I quit GLCSC. But I gave a hundred thousand dollars to their alcoholism treatment program in my grandfather's name, and they're using the money to start the Tessel Alcoholism Rehabilitation Center!" Tess laughed aloud. "That should have started him spinning in his grave. He'll be a whirling dervish by the time I'm done with his money."

It was my job to make sure that time didn't come any too soon. I thought of Lotto winners who'd died penniless and miserable. My mind drifted to GLCSC and all the AA meetings I'd been to there, and all the fundraisers Anne had dragged me to as her escort.

The last time I'd visited GLCSC I'd had to park four blocks away and walk past a couple of street people who seemed to be contemplating where I'd stashed my wallet and how much resistance I'd give. They let me pass, apparently put off by my height. At six feet, I don't seem to suffer from the invisibility and vulnerability a lot of older women say they experience.

Absentmindedly I said, "What GLCSC really needs is another parking lot."

"You're right! I could buy it for them! You think they could get an adjacent lot for a hundred grand?"

"Hey! I was just dreaming aloud. Think about it a while."

"Okay." She looked out the window for a second. "I thought." She scribbled a check and found an envelope and stamp in her burgundy leather briefcase-shaped purse. She jotted some words on a yellow Post-it — "For a new parking lot" — and stuck it on the check. "Be on the lookout for a mailbox."

"You're kidding! Does your accountant know you

do things like this? Send the thing certified mail at least. Maybe you'd better wait a few days, talk to somebody else. You should talk to the GLCSC board — maybe they already have plans for a parking lot. Maybe they need the money more for another program. Besides, a hundred thousand won't buy diddly in Hollywood anymore. The land's too valuable to just hold a parking lot, even if they could get something close by."

Tess licked the envelope and smiled at me. "It's a start. If they need more, they'll call."

I hoped Kitt didn't find out about this impulse and think I should have stopped it. I was supposed to keep Tess to a budget, not give her ideas for wild spending sprees.

I'd have to watch what I wished for aloud — Tess was liable to whip out that checkbook. On second thought . . . I dallied with the idea of mentioning a dream home in Malibu.

We detoured off the freeway to the next small town and hunted down its post office, getting in the door just before closing. Tess spotted a Holiday Inn at the next exit. The suite was a few steps up from the Super Eights and Motel Sixes Hayley and I had used in our frenzied trip six weeks earlier.

I loved the way Tess insisted we go swimming at the motel's indoor pool. I took out the stitches in my left foot with tweezers and alcohol before we went down, figuring the chlorine would kill any germs that might be waiting to invade.

Tess didn't care a bit about the sneers and glares a large-sized woman gets in a bathing suit. Hers was a one-piece bright flowered medley of teals and rust shades. She'd frolicked in Kitt's pool every spare moment. I hadn't imagined the need to pack a bathing suit, so at one of the hotel's shops I bought a modest steel-blue maillot, the last one they had left over from summer. The suit's color set off my hair, which started turning silver in my teens.

I'm in pretty good shape due to my enforced regimen of an hour's run with Radar almost every morning. It isn't as easy to get up for that run the older I get. I had to repulse a couple of geezers who thought I was the answer to their prayers. Tess chuckled at my annoyance.

"You'd think that turning fifty would bring some relief from that crap," I said, wiping water from my eyes. There had to be some advantage to growing older. I didn't seem to have a hell of a lot more wisdom with my years.

"Gain eighty pounds — that'll do it," she laughed. But even she had to fight off one persistent male in a business suit who came over to the pool.

"Asshole," she yelled at him as she did a deliberate bellyflop into the pool that drenched him. "Goddamned chubby chaser." He looked puzzled and finally went away. This time I laughed.

That night, after our swim, I lay in one of the motel room's extra-firm queen-sized beds and couldn't sleep. Tess was out cold in the other. I'd noticed that the hotel's cocktail lounge was open until two a.m. It was one-nineteen a.m.

Except for one night when I'd ended up at L.A. County General as the day's teaching lesson on alcohol overdosing, I'd been sober for nearly twenty years, and another year and a half since then. But the cravings stay right there, in your face. One AA prayer is for that urge to go away, and sometimes it does, for long periods. It wasn't as if every second of every minute I was in agony or anything. Just once in a while the taste of a White Russian comes back, like the ex-smoker who doesn't know what to do with her hands after a good meal. Or whatever.

Dutifully I followed AA guidelines and analyzed how strong the pull was. It didn't seem to go away with thoughts of Tahiti. I could call Mara — it was eleven-nineteen L.A. time — but the craving wasn't that bad. I could handle it.

The AA Blue Book was out in the Cherokee, in the suitcase that also held my computer manuals and assorted miscellaneous. I put my jeans and a sweatshirt back on, over the long T-shirt I sleep in when I'm sharing a room but not a bed, and went out to the car. Deliberately I brought no money or credit cards in case I was pulled toward the bar on my way out.

Radar was ecstatic. I took her for a quick walk and kept her on the leash while I dug out the AA bible. None of the addicts' biographies apply to me, and then again they all do. I keep waiting for a lesbian alkie to write our own AA book, though she'd find it hard to get it approved by AA's hierarchy. I don't go to meetings a lot now for a couple of reasons, one being that I think the Twelve Steps can demoralize a woman who already feels powerless and unable to control her own life. It's not just demon alcohol she has to fight. But AA's the best program we've got so far. Some of the people who've tried to reform it have had their own hidden agendas.

I read until the dashboard clock said it was past closing time.

Finally I could relax.

And now I was having other urges.

Out of wishful thinking, in one of my suitcases I'd packed the peach-colored vibrators Hayley had left behind in L.A., from our visit to the Pleasure Chest when it had become obvious to both of us that an affair was inevitable. She'd told me that she felt bound to practice safer sex because there was a slight chance she was HIV positive. She'd blacked out on the streets before going back to the Betty Ford Center.

First tests were negative, a good sign, but the six months' window time was not yet up before she could feel more sure she was okay. You have to rely on what the scientists say, but always there's that worry that they're wrong.

I'd resisted giving in totally to the dental dams and artificial equipment then, though I'd eventually learned that even safer sex can be sultry and satisfying, especially when it involves Saran wrap and apricot yogurt.

It can also be solitary.

I dug for the vibrators and found my trusty favorite. Unfortunately, it requires an electrical outlet. But Hayley had chosen a variety of sizes and shapes, and the batteries still worked.

No one was around at this hour, and I'd parked the car in a remote part of the parking lot anyway so that Radar wouldn't bark at anyone passing by. Radar would let me know if anyone came near. I locked the door and slipped down low in my seat.

Some urges you don't have to resist.

* * * * *

I let my mind take me to San Francisco. Drums. Sirens. Speakers entreating us to love one another. A hundred thousand aroused anti-war demonstrators doing just that. Woodstock with picket signs.

On stage, Hayley was weaving, writhing, undulating to the drums, searching the audience for something, someone. She spotted me and stopped, mid-beat, then began her sensual dance again, this time facing only me. She gave her hips an extra thrust in my direction, taunting me. She deliberately shimmied, leaning low so that I could see a good deal of those famous breasts which had undeniably helped her young career escalate so fast. So one woman in a thousand is actually built the way the image says we all should look. Hayley was that one in a thousand.

I watched, cheeks burning, my gaze locked with hers. She didn't look away. Her audience was now only me.

I stood, mesmerized, oblivious to the crowds, as they were to us, all of them locked in their own personal universes, while Hayley and I lived in another.

Stealing my glance away for a second, I sighted a dense grove of trees to the left of the crowd. Hayley's pale blue eyes followed mine. She nodded imperceptibly.

Her arm shot into the air, an apparent signal to the backup band to wind it down. One last pulsating crescendo. I turned and made my way toward the shrubbery.

I found a tiny grass-carpeted glen, warmed by sunshine, hidden by shrubs. I waited as she said good-bye to the crowds and a scheduled speaker took the microphone. I could hear none of the macro words, listening only for the micro sounds of breaking twigs and rustling grass.

In a few minutes I heard her coming. She brushed aside the leaves and branches and stood before me. Defiant, challenging. Open. An amazon who had spotted her prey.

She took one more step forward and leaned into me as my arms went around her waist and hers around my neck. She smelled of cherries and leather. Her strong back was damp. I felt the moisture pooling between my legs.

Her breasts were warm and firm against my chest, my nipples tingling at the pressure of her body on mine. Our mouths touched lightly, but only for a second before her lips pressed against mine, hard, then opened with mine. She was hungry for me, her tongue plunging deep into my mouth.

My hands roamed to her solid backside. I kneaded her flesh, pressing her closer and closer to me. I rubbed against her, our thighs directing the centers of our universe to meld into one.

I brought my hands up to her leather bra and undid the clasp. The bra popped loose.

She hunched her shoulders forward so that the bra fell to the grass between us. I stroked those bountiful breasts that were so large for her slender body and let myself suckle at her hard nipples, my face slipping in her sweat. Her hands clasped at my back, dug into my hair, clutched at my arms. She broke away from my grasp and bent to take my breasts into her mouth, one at a time, biting to the point of pain. My body was a white-hot triangle of pulsating energy.

I pulled her up and we kissed again, our tongues penetrating to our depths. We writhed together, whispering sounds that never made it into words, until I sank to my knees and pulled her leather shorts to her ankles. She stepped one foot out of the piled clothing and let me spread her legs so that my tongue could plunge inside. Her feet apart, she rested her hands on my shoulders.

Suddenly she put one leg over my shoulder and thrust her pelvis into my face, demanding without words. I held her tight to keep her from falling as she gave up her balance, relinquishing all conscious control. Her body was acting on its own. I took on all her weight, absorbing it into my weightlessness.

She moaned, a fervent cry that could bring strangers into our world to see what was wrong. Nothing was wrong, not in our own universe. There was only us, one, afire.

"Shhh," I whispered from between her warm lips, my mouth against her slippery, wet inner thighs. She bit her other lips to keep in the sounds.

My tongue found her hidden recess again and plunged against its taut nub. The scents of Kahlua and cream and sweet cherries and sweat rose from her, her juices filled my mouth, filling me, satiating me.

Without even being touched, I came as she did, a groan escaping my lips as she cried out and my hand shot to her mouth. Her chest heaved, her breasts rolled.

Her leg slid off of my shoulder and she stepped back onto the grass. Immediately I missed the feel of her body leaning on mine. She sank to her knees and pulled off my jeans and forced my legs apart.

I landed on the ground and she rolled on top of me. The weight of her body was welcome, already familiar. She shifted until she could push her face into my labia. Hot rushes shot through my body. I forced her legs to open so that I could simultaneously bury my head in her light brown thatch, but she arched her back to keep just out of reach, teasing me further, only a few light hairs brushing against my lips. She had other intentions. She made them very clear.

I was on fire. Sweat streamed down my back into the grass. I came again, this time a rolling, deep climax that went on and on as drums beat from the far stage and Hayley Malone made love to me, over and over again. I heard a faint faraway voice in an echo chamber singing of coming together. A hundred thousand people cheered in the background. Hayley Malone and I clung to each other, enveloped as one.

Gradually I became aware of grass and twigs biting into my bare back. There was still a strange humming from the crowd. I reached for my clothes. Where were the humming people? The demonstration was over. Everyone had miraculously left the park. Even Hayley was gone.

I was alone. With the humming.

In a motel parking lot in Michigan. Sitting in my Jeep Cherokee with Radar panting at my side, looking up at me quizzically, her ears rotating in all directions at the buzzing.

My jeans were abuzz. The humming was from the vibrator firmly against my clit. I had so much energy flowing through me I could probably bite down on a light bulb and it would glow.

Sheepishly I took out my extraneous equipment,

wrapped it in a Burger King napkin from the glove compartment and went back to the hotel room. Tess never woke up.

I washed the vibrator and put it in my overnight bag. Tess snored. I took a shower.

A while later, as I started to doze, I wondered, not for the first time, if I was really in love with Hayley. I was very aware that I hadn't said the words to her yet, though she had said "I love you" to me. We had only known each other for a few months, though they were intense, before she decided to stay in Michigan, and we'd been thinking of other things besides courtship. I'd been her bodyguard, not her peer.

After our first passionate but premature encounter in the hot tub, we'd both pulled back — Hayley caught in the trauma of confronting the "ghosts" from her past, me realizing that I shouldn't have had sex so soon with a woman just out of Betty Ford, a woman who was going through too much to really be available for a relationship.

Our initial encounter might even have harmed her, kept her in her old patterns — I'd felt guilty about it at times. She'd been in a catatonic daze through much of her confrontation with her past. She'd been living on the streets when she was doing drugs and alcohol, and her past was a mess of rehab programs that had failed and utopian communes that had fallen apart. I should have waited the full year AA recommends before a newly sober person should attempt a relationship. My AA sponsor at one point had threatened to fire me — talk about a sobering experience.

How much did I really know of her, the Hayley of

today? She'd said she needed time, that she would call when she was ready. That was nearly two months ago. It could take a lifetime to get over all that she'd been through. Was I really willing to wait? Was I stupid to wait?

Maybe I'd never said "I love you" because at some level I knew it was just an infatuation. It was hard to picture Hayley in a twenty-year-long relationship. But there was a chance — she'd found her demon. Not all of us are so lucky as to have our past come so clear to us as had happened to Hayley in this current stab at sobriety. I'd drop her a note with my new address and phone number at the lodge.

As Tess and I drove farther and farther north, the scenery grew greener, and lakes and rivers became commonplace. Not the L.A. River kind of cement-lined ditch, either. The Golden State had to have gotten its name from the parched tan chaparral that was its predominant color much of the year, not from its image as a gold mine for dreamers. I always loved driving north and watching the landscape become lush and verdant.

A few scarlet- and lemon-colored leaves still flamed on the otherwise stark black branches that made mosaic patterns against clear blue skies. At night you could see thousands of stars, and I could feel my lungs expand.

Even in two days, I could sense the change in myself as well, especially when we were outside of the big cities. Besides making fun of the self-important small towns and their city limit signs bragging that they were home of the 1986 Class C high school state volleyball champs, I also began to relax. I quit tensing up whenever a man walked near the car at a stoplight. Kids and older women didn't keep looking over their shoulders when they walked the sidewalks at dusk.

But all the people outside of the big cities were the same shade of white, all the newspapers had the same headlines in the same language, and all the restaurants bore at least one of the deadly warnings: "Home cooking." "Family." "Country Cooking." "Mom's."

Tradeoffs.

"Don't worry, I'm a hell of a cook," Tess said when I complained about the food at yet another Midwest diner. "Remember that extra suitcase I borrowed from Kitt? Before we left I stocked up on spices and stuff from a bunch of little markets in Hollywood. I've got lemon grass, chipotle chiles, coconut milk, couscous, tahini . . . we'll eat well."

Poking at hard fried chicken, I couldn't wait.

When we crossed the Mackinaw bridge and neared the western side of the Upper Peninsula, the pine-covered hills grew higher.

"Not hills — they're mountains in these parts, and don't you forget it," Tess teased.

"The San Diego freeway into the Valley goes over bigger foothills than these." I snorted. "People ski down these things? Blink and you're at the bottom."

"Give it a rest — some runs are a mile long. This

is the best skiing in the Midwest. You can go skiing every night if you want."

"If you say so. I haven't done that much skiing — I wasn't that good at it," I admitted. "I always felt too tall."

"You! You should see me on skis! I bounce down the hills. But I do love snowmobiling. Wait till you try it."

I could see that the tiny towns were geared up for the ski trade. A sign for a used snowmobile, "xcell nt con iti n, $1,500," made me think I'd stumbled onto the set for "Northern Exposure." I pictured k.d. lang zipping across the ice in *Salmonberries*. I could actually feel myself getting a little excited about the prospects. And I hadn't thought about Hayley for at least an hour.

CHAPTER FIVE

Out of my daydreaming I caught sight of a careening truck weaving out of its lane, coming up fast behind us. I got us off onto the shoulder quick, the Jeep's tires spinning on the gravel.

"What in hell is that!" I screamed. The pickup that had almost sideswiped us had two dead deer tied to its fenders, the deers' tongues sticking out like grape Popsicles. The driver mouthed the M-F words as he passed.

"Your mothers would love it, and so would I," Tess shouted back at them, her words not as easily decipherable through two panes of glass as theirs had been.

"How gross," I said. "The deer, I mean."

"It must be hunting season." Tess seemed to take the carnage in stride. "These small towns depend on hunting for tourist dollars. Think of a deer herd as Disneyland."

"No, thanks."

She glanced over at me and shrugged. "Yeah, most hunters are just pricks who get a kick out of luring deer with fifty-pound sacks of culled carrots. But some people do need the meat. Unfortunately, they're the ones who can't afford the hunting licenses, which cost a lot. When Old Man Tessel died and the lodge closed, the biggest job source for Beer Barrel dried up. The major employer for the whole Upper Peninsula was Sawyer Air Force base, and it's being closed. That hurts, too." She nodded toward a roadside billboard showing a hand of sequinned playing cards. "Next biggest employer is the casinos run by the Sault Ste. Marie Chippewas."

I debated bringing up a discussion on whether casinos were good or bad for Native Americans and decided it wasn't our place to make that decision anyway, so I let Tess talk.

"Mainly the economy is based on the lakes, hills and waterfalls. People who own tourist-oriented businesses can do very well."

She motioned out the window at a sprawling brick ranch home with its own pond and a forty-foot motor home on its immaculately groomed lawn. The next two luxurious homes could have been plucked from West Los Angeles.

But a half-mile down the road was an ancient

aluminum house trailer apparently serving as home to a half-dozen children and an equal number of mixed-breed dogs and rusted car hulks out on the sparse lawn. Someone had chosen an assortment of ceramic ducks and a curvaceous frog in a yellow polka dot bikini for the porch decor. Must be a Michigan state law that every working-class home have ceramic lawn decorations.

"A lot of people work in tourism during summer and fall. If they can't get on with a ski lodge, they live off of unemployment until the checks run out, then go on welfare until spring." Tess looked over at my scrunched-up nose. "Hey, it's a living. The people prefer to make a buck. I don't think I'll get any resistance at all to a lesbian festival — as long as I keep spending money. Just about everybody in town loves me already."

Maybe I rejected the images we were encountering because they were part of what I deliberately left behind when I fled to California, I thought.

"You're probably right," Tess agreed when I told her. "I've got mostly good memories of my past. My mother left U of M in nineteen fifty-five with a wad of money from my father and went out to San Francisco and became a true beatnik, just as Old Man Tessel always said she was. She hung around City Lights bookstore and wrote some awful poetry and met a good Jewish man who didn't care that she had a kid, and they got married."

"True beatnik."

Tess grinned. "Yeah, well, it was the fifties. Men could be lifelong rebels. Women still had to raise the kids and keep house and enable their men. My father sent money every so often, not formal child support, but big chunks whenever he maneuvered something past the old man. Big enough that my mother wanted to keep it coming, so she didn't let her husband adopt me. David Cutler, that's his name. A good man. A claims adjuster for TransAmerica. I called him father, but I always knew there was something different about our relationship. I was nine when Mom told me the truth."

She looked at her map and pointed out my next turn.

"I never got to meet Rick Tessel, though he sent me a few notes on greeting cards for events like my graduations. I was in limbo all my life. That's why I started to go to therapy, and why I finally went back for my master's in counseling. I can relate to people who feel like you do. Like I do."

After a lengthy pause, she said slowly, "I don't think I was cut out to be a therapist. I kept identifying too much with my clients. It's hard for me to be objective, and to not get too hurt when somebody messes up despite everything I've done. You can't make people do what's good for them just by explaining it clearly enough, and I think that's what I had in mind when I started psychology classes. And when *I* have to be strong, I still feel like it's all an act."

I glanced over at her and she shrugged.

"I'd tell my clients that this was a normal feeling, that you make the decisions to *act* strong and eventually you *become* strong. Act as if."

Hayley had said that Synanon, the now-defunct drug rehabilitation program that was so controversial in the seventies, had used the same phrase for one of her attempted dry-outs. Like whistling in the dark to convince yourself you're not afraid. Or wearing a red power jacket to give a speech. Saying "Nice doggie" to the Rottweiler. Act as if.

"But somehow the transformation never really happened with me," Tess said. "I can be the toughest broad around, but inside I'm still quaking."

I thought a minute. "Something a little different happens to me," I finally said. "I tend to sit back and watch myself in a situation, like I'm not really there, like it's a cardboard character down there on earth going through the motions. I had some therapy and found out that this is a good distancing tool, a very safe position to take."

"Alcoholic parents, right?"

"Right." How did she know? Each of us neurotics likes to think that we're unique. Therapists must get awfully bored. I voiced the thoughts. She smiled, nodding.

Oh hell, I hadn't been to an AA meeting in a while. This discussion might do for a substitute.

I stated my hard-earned summary of my life's work: "I have to force myself to be in the situation and do something, say something, instead of sitting back and letting things happen to me."

"Instead of letting the elephant walk around in the living room while nobody says a word." Tess smiled knowingly. "It's typical 'Adult Children of Alcoholic Parents' stuff. It's also what happened with you and Anne." It was a statement, not a question.

"Yeah, I guess. And the resentments built up until I had to get out of there."

"When you could have done something about the problem all along by saying what you felt."

"Oh, probably." A pain rippled through my gut.

"Thank you, doctor." I forced a smile. "You probably aren't as bad of a therapist as you think you are."

"Maybe. But that was a different life. Now I'm Tess Cutler, independently wealthy."

"And you can do any damned thing you want to and people have to like it, right? 'Cause you're rich, rich, rich!"

She play-slugged me in the arm and tipped an imaginary hat. "Smile when you say that, pardner."

CHAPTER SIX

As we approached Ironwood, she pointed out the houses of service people she'd hired for various tasks during the past summer. Most of them had some kind of sign, often misspelled, on their lawn or mailbox advertising their services: "Sam, Your Only Plummer Man." "Emil The Able Roofer." "Lucky's Locksmith Servises."

Erickson, Johannson, Peterson. "Swedish?"

"Finnish. Quite a few Finns were among the lumberjacks who leveled Michigan's virgin white pine forests last century. These trees are new growth.

Then came the miners. When the U.P. was stripped, everybody left. Until tourism became a factor."

"All I've ever heard about Finland is that the people are supposed to be depressed," I said. "Stereotype?"

"They must have cheered up when they got to Michigan. Yeah, stereotype, though Finns are pretty reserved. You'll get a kick out of this. There's a local television show that comes on CBS every Sunday morning called 'Finland Calling' — home movies of visits to Finland. Everybody loves the show, Finnish or not. Then there's this imaginary newspaper columnist character named Heikki, who keeps calling for the establishment of a 'National Poachers Hall of Fame.' People have a weird sense of humor up here."

"I guess." I watched the landscape go by. The average U.P. home had at least one boat and often a small R.V. in its yard, a satellite dish or giant TV antenna, three metal monarch butterflies of graduated sizes decorating the garage, and a huge stack of firewood.

We saw a few people out by the road getting their mail, usually out of battered silver mailboxes on tilted metal posts. Tess honked and waved at several of them. They mouthed, "Hi, Tess!" with big smiles on their bundled-up faces.

"It's like you're a hero."

"When you give somebody a pretty big piece of change, you are," she said. "Though the Beer Barrel Chamber of Commerce guy doesn't agree. He says he's looking at the long-range future of the area. He says having a bunch of man-hating ball-busters around is going to drive off business and families."

"So have you busted his balls yet?"

She merely grinned. "I think he's a Mormon, into that survivalist thing, storing up a couple years' nonperishable goods. I saw him at the Kmart picking up a carton of dehydrated meals sealed in foil envelopes, designed for backpackers, and he doesn't look like a backpacker to me. His name's Joe Underwood. He could be real trouble down the line. You'll meet him, unfortunately."

I swerved to miss a raccoon in the road and we watched it scurry into the brush, bandit eyes glaring at us.

"There's a lot of loners out in the backwoods, people who believe in live and let live. A lot of survivalists hide out in the cabins in the hills, and more than our fair share of loonies. I heard that a few shots were taken at the last census workers."

A long-tailed, ring-necked, jewel-toned pheasant — Tess said they'd been imported from China to supplement the over-hunted native Michigan bird — kicked up a cloud of dust on the road's shoulder, digging for bugs.

Tall pines, winding mountain roads, an occasional small waterfall cascading through carved multi-hued sandstone into rushing streams. Eagles, hawks and owls gliding across a royal blue sky spotted with white puffs of clouds.

"Look! A deer!" I said. The stubby-antlered buck peered at us from a field of harvested corn.

"One of the newspapers had a contest to pick a motto for the state's license plates, and that was one of the most common suggestions," Tess said.

"What?"

"*Look! A deer!*"

We both laughed.

"The lodge was in pretty bad shape when I first saw it," Tess said after a while. "When Old Man Tessel died in nineteen eighty-nine, it was closed down. A few years of Michigan winters can be hard on an unheated, unattended building. There's a caretaker, Rudy Braun, who's been with the place since Noah. His wife used to be the cook before she died. Their kids worked here summers — it was a real family affair." She sank into thought. "I hate to say this, but he just isn't competent. He's utterly useless, worse than useless. Sometimes I think he messes up deliberately to get my goat. He's always looking at me funny. Probably he's never worked for a woman before. Certainly not for an open dyke."

"Is he old enough to retire?"

"Hell, his kids are probably old enough to retire."

"Is he on Social Security?"

"It's been taken out of his checks as far back as I could find, and I know Tessel had a pension plan for his employees. I don't know why he's still working anyway. I worry that he's got no place else to go."

"You mentioned kids."

"Yeah, he said something once about a daughter in Silver City, a little town the other side of the Porcupine Mountains, and a son in Dearborn. Grandkids, of course. Probably great-grandkids, even great-great-grandkids." Tess paused in thought, then continued, "The daughter would be the one to take him in. It's always the daughter who gets stuck with elder care."

I wondered if my father was still in Florida, still living with some bimbo. I hoped he'd marry one young enough to survive him so that he'd never end up on my doorstep. Higher Power, forgive me for wishing a bad life on another woman, bimbo or not.

Besides, he'd prefer Skid Row to living with his dyke daughter, afraid I'd treat him the way he treated me.

"And I keep thinking I need this guy, because he's the only one who knows all there is to know about the lodge." Tess's voice brought me back to Beer Barrel. "But he keeps messing me up."

"How?"

"Oh, I told him to have the bathrooms converted to handicap access. Even without the Americans with Disabilities Act, I'd want to do it anyway. Take out the urinals, put in at least one large-sized stall with railings and a lower sink with lever faucets in each bathroom, I told him. He had plumbers come in that did that." Another of Tess's sighs. "But he didn't have them enlarge the doors so a wheelchair can get through. It cost me a mint to go in afterward and have the bathrooms redone."

"Unless you have something in writing — like the specs — that's not enough to fire him for."

"There's more. He said he misunderstood my request that he repair all the screens for the porch — he burned them instead! I'm sure I was clear. I think he did it on purpose. So then I had to have new custom-made screens built, which cost me another mint."

"I thought you didn't mind spending money."

"I don't, on a good cause. I hate to waste it though." Another sigh. "And it's going to be awkward to have a male employee around during the music festival. I won't be a sexist and fire him because he's

71

a man or because he's old. Not to mention it's illegal. I just don't know what to do. I don't like being a boss." There was a bit of a pout to that Lucille Ball face.

So it's true therapists all have their own neurotic quirks. I'd fired so many employees in the days when I was a drunk that I didn't think twice about it. I thought about them plenty when I did my AA inventory of all the people I'd hurt in my life. This Rudy sounded like he'd legitimately earned his ticket out of town. But she was right, for both legal and ethical reasons, we'd have to be very careful in how we handled Rudy. A thought occurred to me. "Maybe you could give him a paid vacation during the festival."

She brightened at the idea. "Oh, thank you, Laney! I knew you were a life-saver! You're going to solve all my problems, I know it."

Once again I fought off the feeling that I'd taken on a job that I wasn't sure I could handle. Mentally I tallied all the mistakes I might make if I didn't watch out. This promotion wasn't exactly boosting my self-esteem.

My Higher Power finally got a word in edgewise. She told me to knock it off and concentrate on doing my best. This time her voice sounded just like Oprah.

CHAPTER SEVEN

"Here we are at beautiful downtown Beer Barrel,"
Tess announced. "Pull into that station for gas."
Radar stirred in the back seat at the car's slowing
and surveyed her surroundings along with us, her big
white ears rotating to catch every sound.

The town should have been called Four Corners —
that's all there was. Not even a stop sign, though
directives on either end of town slowed traffic to
thirty. The gas station did mechanical and body
repair work — "We fix flats and snowmobiles." And it

was also a convenience store with another sign that read:

"Hunting and fishing licenses"
"We serve you."
"Leeches."
"Night crawlers"
"Sandwiches"

I wouldn't be buying any sandwiches. Then I saw the hand-lettered sign underneath it:

"Eat here and get gas and worms."

More of that Finn humor, I gathered.

Across the street, on the northwest corner, was a red brick office building missing a few bricks, with signs for a barber shop, beauty shop, the Beer Barrel Chamber of Commerce, and an American Legion post, all operating out of one storefront.

The rest of the stores in the building were empty, their windows boarded up or soaped over. A man and a woman, both sixty-something, sipped coffee and stood looking out the barber shop window at us, the only action in town.

Even from a distance I could see that the man was scowling. His pants hung loose on toothpeg legs, but his face had three chins, draped crosswise from his lower lip to his collar like three creases in a beige neckerchief. His round cheeks mounded high like scoops of ice cream. He could have been pregnant, based on the small round belly that pouched over the waistband of his gray slacks, tugging at the lower buttons of his crisp white shirt. You couldn't tell from looking at his own nonexistent hair if he was a good barber.

"That's Joe Underwood," Tess said. "The Chamber of Commerce guy I told you about? The woman's his wife, Ardith. She's the town's only beautician. Can't do a fade worth a damn. No unisex haircuts in Beer Barrel, by golly."

Each white strand of Ardith's hair was curled in its own direction and plastered in place. At least she hadn't tinted it blue. Her royal blue cotton blazer jacket over a white blouse and black polyester stretch pants made her look like a uniformed welcome hostess for Wal-Mart. So this was the town's leading couple. Oh yeah, a music festival would fit right in.

On the southwest corner was Waldrun's Bakery, Coffee Shop and Fine Dining, all one establishment, sharing a wall with the Dew Drop Inn. A giant doughnut painted onto the front window invited passersby to the bakery, while a neon depiction of the Superior Beer moose mascot welcomed thirsty travelers and bored residents to the bar.

I wondered how they'd react to a few hundred wild women, in town for Tess's music festival, dancing to the jukebox, no matter how well they tipped and how diligently they kept their shirts on.

Through the plate glass windows I could see the sole waitress, a natural blonde pony-tailed anorexic, walking through a swinging half-door between the bar and the restaurant, apparently bringing a tray of beers over to the lunch crowd — three flannel-shirted men around a wooden table, chomping into thick sandwiches. I hoped Waldrun's didn't get its sandwiches from across the road.

The men all looked at the waitress's nonexistent butt as she went back into the kitchen.

The Beer Barrel Post Office, another boarded-up store front, a fire station big enough to hold maybe one fire truck, and two churches held down the remaining corner. Two hundred feet farther down the road was another building that had apparently been empty so long I could get no idea what it had once held.

One church was True First Baptist, describing itself on its peeling white wooden sign as "Independent Fundamentalist King James Version 1611, the Rev. Mark Hudspeth, pastor." The sign also gave the times for Bible study, youth night and seven weekly prayer services.

"Do they have any time left to cause trouble?" I wondered aloud.

"Hudspeth? He's a corker. I went to a village council meeting when I first arrived and introduced myself. This guy thought he brought his pulpit with him. I got a sermon that would have made Jerry Falwell proud. Lumpy guy in shiny suits, combs his hair in circles to hide the bald spot. He's trouble, too."

Brass letters on the side of the second church, a yellow brick building, said Reorganized Church of Jesus Christ of Latter Day Saints. No further information on any kind of sign anywhere. I guess if you were Mormon you already knew all you had to know.

"There's a Catholic church and a Lutheran church

a little ways down the road," Tess said. "A Father Mullins and a Reverend Koonig. Mullins is here part-time — his main parish is in Ironwood. Both of them seem like pretty good guys. But I don't think any of the churches draws more than thirty people on Sunday." Tess leaned over to my side. "Hi, Thal. I'm back in town. Fill 'er up," she told the gas station attendant. "They still believe in full service here," she said to me. "No extra charge. I suspect it's because Thal's glad for the chance to talk to people. Not to me, of course."

"Down, Radar," I ordered my shepherd, who'd sat straight up and growled at the attendant when he approached the window. She whimpered and went back to her bed — Tess's soft-sider. "Why not to you?" Tess didn't answer.

The man didn't say a word as he briskly pumped gas. In his one-piece brown jumpsuit, smeared with grease, puffy with insulation, he was as rigid as a Buckingham Palace guard and just as silent. The fingers were cut out of his maroon gloves, exposing chapped red digits that matched his weathered red face.

I tried to make eye contact, with no success.

A short man, he looked as if he would creak if he bent over, though he couldn't have been that old. No hair showed under the hood of the jumpsuit, though his eyebrows and eyes were the same dust shade as his complexion. He avoided looking in our direction, staring down the road as if wishing for another car, any other car, to drive in and rescue him.

"Had any more snow while I was gone?" Tess asked him.

Silence. She repeated the question.

Reluctantly he answered. "Two. Melted. Another due. Eleven twenty-eight." His lips barely moved.

She counted out exact change. " 'Bye, Thal. See you again soon."

He didn't reply.

"He didn't even check the oil or clean the windshield." Tess chuckled when he retreated.

"Not everybody loves you." I drove back onto the road. "So why doesn't he like to talk to you?"

"Umm, when I got here last spring, I hired his wife to take down the curtains and drapes throughout the lodge, and we got to talking. A lot. She finally admitted she'd always thought she was a lesbian, and we, umm, got together a few times."

"You nasty recruiter, you!"

Tess's hot pink cheeks clashed with her carrot hair.

"What happened to the wife? What's her name? Is she still around? You didn't tell me about her."

"Her name is Rita Swanson. A natural blonde, built like Martina but Martina never wore a housedress. Rita doesn't either, not anymore."

A quick picture of k.d. lang's love interest in *Salmonberries* popped up again. I wondered if Tess had gone snowmobiling with this Rita.

"The other husbands in town must have loved that. I thought you said everybody liked you. So what happened?"

She shrugged.

"Don't stop now. And? And?"

"And we had a great summer. She left her husband and moved down to Ferndale outside of Detroit, where she found a lesbian roommate from the bulletin board of A Woman's Prerogative bookstore."

"And? Does she come up to see you?"

"She hasn't been back, though we've talked on the phone a few times. She's going to Oakland University now, and she thanks me profusely for helping her escape her life. Only I wish she'd taken a little longer to escape, and not gone so far. There's a lesbian bookstore, Sweet Violets, in Marquette a couple hundred miles from here, and a decent college, and there's a bit of a community in Escanaba south of Marquette. But no, she wanted the big city."

"Did you think about going after her?"

That was a sigh I heard from Tess's direction. Either that or one of my tires had a slow leak.

"Sure, I thought about it. A lot. But her life's not up here anymore, and I guess mine is. What she really wanted was for me to take her back to L.A. She'll probably get up enough guts to go there eventually. Or someplace." Tess was doing an awful lot of sighing. "Coming out totally will take her a few years. Maybe some time in the future we'll get together again. Probably not. It feels over. I'm not sure we had anything in common in the first place. Besides sex."

I could identify. As we drove I told her more about Hayley's need for more time, before starting up with me again and before attempting a singing comeback.

"You need to decide what *you* want from the relationship and go after it, rather than waiting around at her beck and call," Tess said. "You could force the issue, make her take the leap into singing, or admit she doesn't really want to. Or you might realize that she's not ready to try again. Maybe she'll never be ready to try again. Somebody who's lived on the streets might have something deeper to deal with, something four trips to Betty Ford never solved."

Her words stung. I recovered in my usual manner. "Will that be seventy-five dollars, doctor? And are you going to heal yourself?"

"You're right, I should talk. Let Hayley take her own time. No harm waiting. Oh, we're almost to the lodge. Turn here."

We pulled down a one-lane asphalt road and drove for a few miles through nothing but woods, posted with "Keep Out" signs.

"Now turn right," Tess ordered, and we entered a winding gravel driveway marked "Private" that meandered around a small lake. Several other roads took off in different directions through the property. "One end of the lake has a sandy beach for swimming," she said. "Just before I left I found out I had to have it dredged before winter because it needs time to grow back some of the vegetation after dredging. Otherwise I'd have had one hell of an ugly lake next summer for the festival."

"What was wrong with it?"

"Oh, too much algae. I don't think any fish were left either. I'll have it restocked. Strictly panfish for leisurely canoe rides with a bamboo pole and bobbin. Anyone who wants to do serious fishing can take one of the outboards from the garage and drive over to Lake Gogebic or any of the other lakes. The same with Jet Skis and water skis — I want this lake for peace and quiet."

She pointed to the hollow of a small hill on the other side of the lake. "That's where I want to have the music shell built so that women can listen to music while they drift in a canoe or lie around in the sand tanning during the day. Maybe I'll float candles on the lake for night concerts. If I don't have fireflies I'll import them."

"Citronella candles, I hope," I said, remembering Mosquito Lake from my childhood.

Her casual scanning of the landscape came to a halt as her face froze in the direction of the lake, like a bird dog on point. "Shit!" She rolled down the window and stuck her head out, still staring at the lake.

"What's the matter?"

"Do you see that?"

"What am I looking for?"

"A sandy beach that doesn't exist anymore. That goddamn Rudy, he had the dredgers take away the beach too! Can't he get anything right? I *know* I told him to keep the beach and have more sand brought in. I wonder what replacing a beach is going to cost me?" She picked up my phone. "May I?"

"As long as you're paying for it. Those things can eat you alive. I never use mine except for Meyers Music business." My first month's bill, when I had casually enjoyed the phone's novelty, had knocked me off my feet. From then on I'd handed the envelopes to Kitt unopened and had friends call me at home.

"Of course I'm paying for it." She dialed and got no answer. "He must be outside, messing up something else." She kept muttering to herself as we drove along the gravel road. "I'm assuming I *can* get enough sand to rebuild the beach," she was saying half-aloud. Rudy's name kept coming up, interspersed with assorted curses.

"Is that the hunting lodge?" I spotted a log cabin, then noticed it was in a semi-circle of five identical house-sized cabins around a small, square utility-looking building.

"Nope, just one of the outlying cabins." We drove on. I spotted tennis courts, an Olympic-sized swimming pool covered with a blue tarp for the winter, and a huge garage. A hotel-sized satellite dish aimed for the skies.

We rounded a curve and were suddenly in a parking lot big enough for a Safeway. I felt my jaw drop. "Wow! A log cabin Hilton!"

CHAPTER EIGHT

Radar sat up from her sleep and barked. Tessel Hunting and Fishing Lodge loomed like a cross between an L-shaped log cabin and a stone castle, three stories high and a city block wide. A deluxe resort, not the rustic little camp I'd pictured.

Only something about it was strange. "Why such an extreme angle to the roof?"

"They get two hundred inches of snow here in the winter. You need pitched roofs to keep the snow from accumulating and caving in your ceiling."

Two hundred divided by twelve — "My God! Sixteen feet of snow! We're going to be buried alive!"

"It doesn't come all at one time," Tess reassured me. "It evaporates, sometimes there's a thaw, it blows around a lot. The county's highway people clear the main roads pretty fast, and eventually they get around to the back roads. Thal Swanson's brother-in-law, Karl Thorsdal, runs the snow removal service I hired, and he said he'd also cut some snowmobile trails around the property when I ask him to. I'm his biggest customer now so he says he'll always do me first."

"Rita's brother?"

"Yeah."

"Cozy."

"Yeah. He's a real nice guy, he's okay about it. He sees that she's happy now. Anyway, he's a member of some snowmobiling club which grooms the snowmobile trails along the abandoned railroad tracks for the public. The drifts may get pretty deep, but usually there's only a couple of feet on the ground."

Only.

"Sometimes you're cut off for a day or two, but you prepare for it, that's all. Everybody has a week's food in reserve just in case."

Just in case I made it back from this gig alive, I'd need my head examined.

Circling three sides of the first floor was a screened-in porch furnished with small wooden tables and chairs, like the set-up for a giant bridge tournament.

Radar was dancing all over us in her excitement to get out of the Jeep and explore. "Sit," I ordered. She paid me no attention. What was with my dog? I repeated myself with more force. She sat but squirmed and whimpered. I parked next to the only other car in the lot, Tess's red Chevy Blazer four-by-four. She said Rudy had driven her to the local airport when she left for L.A. so that she hadn't had to leave her car in the airport lot unattended. He was supposed to have put it in the garage but he hadn't done that, either.

"I wonder where Rudy's Suburban is?" Tess said. "Maybe he's gone to town. He knew I'd be coming back today."

The far left side of the lodge seemed to be set up for truck deliveries, first-floor and basement level.

"How many rooms does this sucker have?" I choked out.

"I think there's two hundred bedrooms on the second and third level. The first floor is mainly open space that can be divided into meeting rooms, or converted to dining areas, or used as a kind of den with sofas and easy chairs. It could be set up as a cocktail lounge with entertainment. Talent shows, readings, workshops . . . lots of possibilities."

I put Radar on her chain leash and she squatted quickly, then pulled hard to get loose. I could barely hold her. She wanted to run, and she strained and whined as I dragged her toward the lodge. She never acted this way — what was wrong with my damned dog?

Tess let us inside. We stopped first at the porch. Radar's toenails clicked on the wood floor. The frames around the screens were unpainted raw wood.

"Note the brand-new screens, courtesy of Rudy's mistake." Tess grimaced. "He was supposed to have had the frames painted before the temperature went down to freezing. Now I have to wait until spring. Storm windows should be up by now anyway. What's he been doing? I left him a list."

She surveyed the expansive porch and a smile played on her face, her crisply outlined lips making her white teeth seem even brighter. The cold air made her cheeks red, which made her happy eyes look even greener.

"This porch has to be my favorite part of the whole lodge. Can't you see a couple hundred topless dykes out here on a hot night, playing pinochle, sipping lemonade or wine, shmoozing up to one another, table-hopping, with hot music drifting through from the party inside?"

I could.

"Maybe we can serve breakfast out here. You can see where they had small bars every so often on the porch — God forbid the guys should have been fifty feet away from booze. The alcohol and food were cleared out when the place was closed down in 'eighty-nine. I'm keeping a beer and wine license only. I'll have to figure out how to have a 'clean and sober' section of the cabin for non-drinkers."

I had a moment of thankfulness that I wouldn't be stumbling upon a bottle of Kahlua one dark and stormy night.

"I thought I'd add small steam tables where the bars used to be, a serve-yourself breakfast buffet. A couple juices, fruits, cereals, muffins, maybe some bagels, scrambled eggs." She swiped at something buzzing her face. "It's too late in the season for mosquitoes, where'd you come from?" she muttered. To me she said, "We call our local variety Yooper Eagles."

"Yooper?"

"From Upper Peninsula. U.P., Yooper. The mosquitoes and gnats are really bad. We'll have to spray the grounds a lot, and sell a ton of mosquito repellant."

I made a mental note about whether to mention the bug problem in advance PR, for women with allergy problems.

"These wood tables are in pretty good shape." Tess pulled out a chair to show me. "I had some local people give them a fresh coat of white paint and refinish them as needed." The chair looked brand new.

"Inside, a lot of the stuffed furniture was pretty ratty, so I had it hauled away. I ordered a couple new sofas to see what they'd look like in the room before I decided how to furnish it. The dining room stuff was in great shape. The big tables are made of varnished pine."

We entered the main room — the great room, Tess called it. I noticed the heavy wood doors as well as screens, and the thick wood shutters drawn over the windows to the porch.

"Believe it or not, this place is insulated pretty well. We heat with fuel oil — there are a couple of thousand-gallon tanks in the basement — plus there are fireplaces everywhere, including in the best suites on the second floor. Look at that beauty."

You could barbecue a whole steer over the coals from the central fireplace in what was now an open pine-paneled, hardwood-floored room. The center of the great room had a cathedral ceiling three stories high, with the second and third floors railed off like wooden balconies all around.

The chimney, which rose three stories to the ceiling, was of natural stone, a beautiful touch.

"Good grief, what's that!"

I stared up to the second-story level of the chimney. Hanging from it, or somehow built into it, was a metal suspension frame that held a gigantic moose head.

Its glass eyes definitely leered. Radar looked up too and barked like a fool. Her toenails clicked on the polished wood floor as she pranced below the moose, lunging against her leash. I was ready to smack her on her nose.

"That's the Superior Beer mascot." Tess sighed. "Actually, there aren't that many moose in Michigan. They were extinct here for a while, until Michigan started to trade elk for moose with Ontario and a few small herds got started again. But there's that damn moose head lording it over everything."

She glared at it. It smirked at her.

"I tried every way possible — it can't be taken down. To exert enough force to cut through the metal could cause the chimney to topple. It's built into the structure — at least that's what they tell me. What do you think?"

"I think it's hideous. Can't you at least put a drape over it?"

"Too close to the chimney heat. Somehow they put something flameproof on the back of the moose so it isn't hurt by the heat, but nobody I've hired has been able to figure out what to do with the thing."

I could picture unsuspecting lesbian animal rights activists arriving for a concert, taking one look at the moose and running for home. Or setting up picket lines.

"You're going to have to tell people about it from the start, so no one's taken by surprise," I suggested.

"Let me think. It was a mascot, so we'll make it our own. Some slogan about the patriarchy — like 'Off with its head.' We'll think of something. It'll go in the brochure."

"You're so clever!" Tess said, giving me a hug. "I've been worrying what to do about it."

I eyed the moose. The moose eyed me. Radar continued to growl and bark and yank at her leash.

Another idea hit me. "Hey, what about Bullwinkle? We can set up a VCR underneath running Bullwinkle cartoons. We can give funny names to different areas of the lodge and this'll be the Bullwinkle Pen."

"Great!" Tess turned her attention elsewhere, apparently satisfied that we'd solve the problem of the moose. "What do you think of the sofas?"

Forcing myself away from the moosehead's stare, I looked at the samples Tess had strewn around the living room. Even to my eyes, each of them was all wrong. Too flowery, too small, too over-stuffed, too plain . . . She'd picked the best of the lot, a camel corduroy lounger, for in front of the fireplace.

"I think you're going to need some pieces of size in here so they're not lost," I said. "You need to think about traffic patterns and conversation groupings and materials that stand up to the weather and crowds. The wisest thing to do is to hire an interior decorator, somebody who specializes in hotels and lodges. It'll be cheaper in the long run."

"You're probably right." Tess sniffed. "I didn't like any of these pieces when I got them in place. So what am I going to do with them?"

"If you don't want to return them, we can see if they fit into any of the suites or the outlying cabins. Let the decorator decide. If worse comes to worst, you could donate them to charity. You're probably being eaten alive by the IRS."

"Good idea!" Tess gave me a quick hug. I'm not one for that kind of spontaneity, but it felt good. "I knew I did the right thing signing up with Meyers Music. Okay, now for the upstairs."

Tess guided me to one of the two broad-beamed wooden staircases in the great room.

"Do you think you can get an elevator in here for wheelchairs and women who can't climb stairs?" I asked.

"One's on order, coming in the spring, custom-made for that alcove. Rudy did do that much."

"Where is he anyway?"

"I've got no idea. He'll show up. Unfortunately."

Upstairs Tess swept open door after door, stopping finally at the rooms in the rear, which I figured were over the meeting rooms on the first floor. I could see a smaller metal stairwell, apparently for employees to service the upper floors.

I wondered if the lodge had had room service. Undoubtedly. There was something that looked like a bank of dumbwaiters built into the rear wall, at a place that I calculated was above the first-floor and basement kitchens.

"This is Rudy's room," Tess said, knocking on one door. "Asshole," I barely heard her say. Aloud, she called, "Rudy?" No answer. "He knew I'd be back today. We'll meet him later."

She moved on to a small hall with two doors. "This is where the Tessels stayed. This suite's mine, and I thought you might want the one next door. The heating is on zones, so I pretty much live in this area and the kitchen and main room downstairs now that it's getting cold. It's wasteful to heat the whole place."

"Where do you work?" I asked.

"There are four small offices downstairs by the big meeting room, but I've been working out of my bedroom suite. You can either set up your office downstairs or do the same. It would be more convenient if you worked upstairs too, but it's up to you. I know some people can't relax in a room if it's also used for work."

Radar and I glanced into our new quarters. Mostly I liked it. Varnished pine log walls and hardwood pegged floors. King-sized bed with blue plaid wool bedspread, leather couch and easy chairs, large-screen TV and stereo in a pine entertainment center carved with an oak-leaf and acorn design, pine desk with a hutch that would hold a computer, phones both at the desk and in the bathroom, good lighting, a window and windowseat with a view of white pines and the lake, Navajo-inspired thick wool area rugs in unauthentic shades of royal blue that went with the bedspreads and curtains. Microwave, refrigerator and wet bar. I checked — no airline-sized bottles of booze or cellophane-wrapped crackers in the fridge. The desk was big enough for a couple of weeks' work, maybe with an additional file cabinet brought in to hold all the brochures and contracts I expected to accumulate.

The artifacts in the room were something else. A wood-carved mallard decoy on the fireplace mantel, a taxidermist's version of a trout on the wall, a horseshoe over the door. A totally useless sixteenth-century version of a globe on the coffee table. The backdrop for an L.L. Bean catalog shoot.

I hummed the tune to "Macho Man." Wait until a woman decorator got done in here.

Radar sniffed in the corners and under the bed and again strained to get loose. I held on to her leash for all I was worth. Too many male smells, maybe.

"Besides the dozen suites, about half the rooms have their own bathrooms while the other hundred share dormitory-style baths down the hall."

She showed me one of the smaller rooms. Still nice.

"There's this crazy song from a group called Da Yoopers — sort of the mascots of the Upper Peninsula," Tess said as we went from room to room. "They've got a song called 'The Second Week of Deer Camp,' about a bunch of smelly, unshaven, drunken louts hanging around a log cabin playing poker and drinking beer. They haven't even been out to look for deer yet and it's already their second week at deer camp. You'll have to hear it to believe it."

I feigned horror.

"That's the typical image of deer hunters. But these were the upscale kind. Old Man Tessel's father was good friends with Henry Ford and all the mining and logging barons, and they met here a lot in the early part of the century. Ford, Firestone, Rockefeller,

Edison . . . a lot of the richest people in the world walked these same floors."

I pictured the dictatorial Henry Ford I'd seen in pictures pounding a fist on a meeting room table below.

"Later on, Ford owned his own hotel farther east," Tess said, "near the sawmill he built to provide lumber for his flivver plant. The mill ran until Ford died in 'forty-seven."

"You mean like wood for the sides of station wagons?"

"Nope, the actual internal structures were originally made of wood, until the carmakers switched to steel."

"You're certainly a fount of information," I teased her.

"Nothing else to do nights but hole up with a bunch of books from the Ironwood library. There was a famous writer from around here, John Voelker, who wrote *Anatomy of a Murder*. He said if it hadn't been for U.P. winters he would have never written a book."

Two hundred inches of snow. Maybe I'd write one too.

"I found out there were a lot of these huge lodges up here in the early part of the century. For all the auto barons and lumber barons and mining barons and newspaper barons. I'm sure they broke every part of the Sherman Anti-Trust Act when they got together."

She scraped at a piece of darkened wood and apparently decided it wasn't a problem.

"Big politicians came around too — plenty of smoke-filled rooms in this joint. Some members of the

Michigan Senate and not a few Congressmen called this their second home. If these walls could talk . . ."

So we were standing in a piece of Michigan history. We were about to rewrite it.

Suddenly Radar broke free and took off at a dead run down the stairs, toenails clicking on the varnished floors, her chain leash flopping uselessly behind her, clinking on each step.

"Radar!" I screamed.

From the top of the stairs we saw her race for the front door and frantically edge it open with her paws. And she was gone. By the time I got downstairs she was out of sight.

"No sense going after her — she could be anywhere in these woods," Tess pointed out. "She'll come back when she's ready."

"Yeah, maybe. She doesn't know the area. We haven't tracked our smell around for her to follow back. And her leash could catch on something and choke her to death."

"Has she ever done this before?"

"No, never . . ." But then I remembered our visit to Michigan with Hayley. "Yes, she did run away last time. She took off chasing a deer and didn't come back for hours."

"But she did come back."

"That time. Hayley said something about it being against the law for a dog to run deer, and that the fine was two thousand dollars, plus the dog gets shot on sight?"

"I think I heard that too," Tess said. "Maybe we'd better drive around and look for her."

CHAPTER NINE

We scrambled back into the Jeep and drove every inch of gravel road and rutted path of the thousand-acre grounds. The front driveway was not the only access road onto the property, and we drove up and down the feeder roads as well, anyplace Radar might have reached running at full speed in the time that had elapsed. The place was a maze. Even Tess got lost a couple of times.

"These back roads aren't on the map," she said when we were staring at one more apparent dead end. "I think they're old logging trails." No sign of the white German shepherd.

"There's more land we can search next door. The Tessel Foundation owns the adjoining property that's used for one of those paintball clubs — those places where men go to play pretend-survivalist games?"

I stared at Tess. "I read about the concept, but didn't pay much attention. Now that you mention it, these places have been on news shows off and on. I tuned the stories out as something I'd never need to know about." I sniffed. "I could have gone my whole life not being next door to a survivalist camp."

"I think this one is more just a fun place where men go off on sort of retreats where they play combat soldiers against one another, only they use guns that shoot paint capsules. I think they compete in teams."

"I can't believe men take this stuff seriously."

"Really! If you get shot, you get splattered with paint and you're out of the game. Guys pay big bucks for this stuff. You see 'L.A. Law' the night they had that little tax attorney jumping around in the bush playing Conan the Barbarian?"

Had to pass there. I'm not much for following a TV series — too many of them seem like glorified soap operas. Too many nights when I'm away. I lose the continuity you need to really enjoy them.

"Anyway, Old Man Tessel had some of his money tied up in this charity foundation which is kind of self-perpetuating, and one of the things it owns is this Camp Tessel next door. Go back to the main road and I'll show you how to get there."

I noticed that a chain link fence started at the

end of the hunting lodge property and ran back into the woods, clearly a dividing line between the two businesses. "The fence doesn't go all the way back," Tess said. "They don't like to stop the movement of the animals. This used to be one piece of acreage, way back when. The foundation put the fence in about as far back as a hunter would go on foot." The eight-foot fence, topped with barbed wire, also ran alongside the road with "Keep Out" signs every few hundred feet. As far as I could tell, the entire U.P. was posted.

The next gravel road after the one leading to the lodge had a wooden sign painted in camouflage colors: "Camp Tessel." The chain link fence indented to accommodate about thirty feet of driveway into the road and a parking lot for maybe forty cars. Only a white Land Rover was in the lot.

The fence ran up to a small one-story red brick building where someone inside controlled the locked gate that stopped traffic into the interior.

Tess got out of the Jeep and rang the doorbell alongside the steel door to the brick building. A camera lens was mounted above the door. She must have met the admittance criteria, for she disappeared into the building.

A minute later she reappeared and the gate swung open. "The manager of the place is a guy named Hank Gerlock," she reported. "He's been really sweet but kind of shy. I met him at the lawyers' office when I was told about the will. He says to look around anywhere we want to."

"Do these guys still play their games during the winter?"

"I think they do winter survivalist games a couple of weekends a year. Anyway, Hank says there's nobody else on the property right now."

"Why is he still there then?"

"He lives here year-round, like a caretaker. When we met at the lawyers' he said something about liking to live away from cities. He hires local people to staff the camp when he's got a group booked. For some reason, he seems to enjoy the paintball thing; he says it gives him a kick. He goes out with the groups himself sometimes, just for the fun of it." She rolled her eyes. "Men."

We scanned the horizon for Radar. Tess talked as we kept looking. "I don't see how Gerlock's got time — he also runs the Tessel Foundation from that office, by the way. He's got his computer hooked up with every online service there is."

"Hey, great, maybe he could help me figure out the Internet. Our e-mail's on Delphi so I know the basics, but I wish I knew more."

Tess shook her head. "I wouldn't ask him. He's a bit of a recluse." I pictured Howard Hughes sitting around growing foot-long fingernails.

Calling out for Radar, we drove down all of the gravel roads past two more log cabin-like buildings, though these seemed more like military fortresses than vacation homes. One chimneyed building looked like a barracks, bunk beds visible through the windows. I gathered that some groups stayed overnight at the camp. Most of the property had no roads, just cryptic signs and brightly colored dots and arrows posted on various trees, high dirt berms and bunkers.

We stopped and peered into some of the cabins.

One of them seemed to be the store. Racks of guns of various sizes were behind locked glass doors in gunmetal-gray painted wood cabinets. Pistols and rifles, both semi-automatics and air pumps, were listed for rent at fifteen to twenty-five dollars a day, or for purchase at seventy to four hundred dollars. They looked like regular guns to me. Eye goggles ran fifteen to sixty dollars.

The gelatin-shelled, water-soluble paintballs themselves were for sale in cases of two hundred to a thousand — forty dollars for the largest case, in any color or assortment, Tess squinted to read the fine print. Don't tell me I'll be needing glasses soon, too. All kinds of camouflage clothes were also available, along with knee and elbow pads, gun barrel squeegees, and items I couldn't even fathom. Paintball was obviously a booming business. I guessed that these mock-military types enjoyed reliving their youth if they'd served, or pretending they were experiencing the real thing if they hadn't.

I looked over at Tess, who shook her head in disgust, too. "Macho Man" kept running through my brain.

Once we'd circled everywhere we could, yelling for my dog, we drove back out. The unseen Hank Gerlock apparently saw us coming and opened the gate. Silently we drove back to the lodge.

One more time I took the Jeep through all of the roads and paths on the property. No Radar. We gave up and returned to the main building and started to unload our suitcases. She'd have to come back on her own. I kept listening for barks and whimpers, jumping at the sound of a dropped toothbrush. I imagined the worst.

"She'll be back," Tess told me. "There are too many wonderful smells to investigate."

"You're probably right, but I have to go back out. I'm going on foot this time. Want to go with me or stay here?"

"Oh hell, I might as well come along. You're likely to get lost without a guide. You may get lost *with* a guide."

Tess dug cowboy boots out of one suitcase and changed from her usual uniform, a jumper worn over a T-shirt, into elastic-waist jeans and a fleece-lined denim jacket.

"You need something more than tennis shoes for this terrain," she warned. "And thick socks. It's cold walking out there."

I found my Timberland chukkas and my old steel-gray leather bomber jacket. We were ready.

Not yet. She put red scarves around both our necks. "Don't walk in the woods in November without bright colors."

"Radar!" I shouted as we traversed the land. No answer. No quick flashes of white in the bush, though there were a few unmoving patches of white that turned out to be unmelted snow left from the first snowfalls.

We circled the small, devastated lake. We investigated the garage, which was filled with snowmobiles, canoes, outboard boats on trailers, waterski jets, riding lawn mowers, tractors and snow blowers. We checked out the five groupings of smaller log cabins, six cabins per cluster around a central restroom and showers, each of the thirty cabins holding eight bunk beds.

But no sign of Radar. I squinted toward the horizon and struck out for the back reaches of the property, Tess breathing heavily behind me.

"Radar!" I yelled again. My voice rebounded in the cool breeze.

In response, a *crack* sound echoed somewhere around us, then another *crack* followed. A puff of dust billowed at my foot.

The trailing echo of the rifle shots lingered like the fading tail of a falling star, or a streaming firecracker. But it hadn't been a firecracker.

"Drop! Those were shots!" I yelled to Tess. We scrambled on our hands and knees toward a fallen log and crawled over it as fast as we could. We landed in a frozen mudhole filled with decomposing leaves. Tess and I huddled in the dirt.

No more shots. We lay there, shaking, listening for any sound, a footstep, for what seemed like forever before we dared to raise our heads and look around.

You learn a lot from movies. I took off my jacket and put it on the end of a long branch and waved it in the air, to draw any more bullets. Silence. We got up slowly.

I was looking around where I had seen one bullet hit the ground when I heard a rustling sound coming through the brush. I nearly jumped out of my skin.

A leaf-covered white mass forced itself through the brush.

"Radar!"

She appeared, laughing and happy, shaking the dirt out of her filthy coat, still dragging her chain leash behind her. I grabbed it and yanked her to me.

It took everything I had to not beat her for running away. Or was it just misplaced fear that made me want to flail away? I hugged her hard instead.

"Don't ever do that again," I ordered, half sobbing in relief. "And why didn't you stop whoever was shooting at us?" I buried my face in her ruff and held on tight.

CHAPTER TEN

The bullet I dug out of the ground was a thirty-ought six, the kind used in most deer rifles, the Gogebic County sheriff, Ron Conkey, said. He drove in from Bessemer a mere three hours after we called. Plenty of time for me to wrestle Radar back into the kitchen where she couldn't possibly force open a door, and then to return to the scene and find the slug.

I'd asked Tess if Beer Barrel had any kind of police officer. "Only Keith Zaurko, a good old boy who has a TV repair business out of his home by day. He patrols the back roads at night during the summer and he's on call the rest of the time. Don't even bother with him — he won't take this seriously."

Neither did Conkey. He unwound his six and a half feet out of the standard Chevy Caprice police car and took charge. The burly man whose face was as red and blotched as a strawberry sundae laughed us off. Radar, from her faraway lockbox, barked in futility at the sound of his mocking voice.

"They missed, didn't they? A bunch of wild and crazy guys out there this time of year, probably drunk as a skunk. If anybody really wanted to get you, you'd be dead."

"The land's posted," Tess pointed out. "Can't you find out who's been trespassing on my property, if you're not concerned about who tried to kill us?"

He ignored that statement as well.

He did puzzle over the fact that there were no markings from the gun barrel on what was left of the bullet. "The guy kept a mighty clean gun," he said. "A real smooth bore barrel. To tell the truth, I'm not even real sure this is a thirty-ought six, from the damage it suffered when it hit. You say you found it in dirt; it should be just about intact." He stared harder at the bullet. "If I didn't know better I'd think this was a smaller diameter shell, something going a lot faster than from a deer rifle. But hey, the rest of it has all the characteristics of a thirty-ought six. Just a deer hunter who maybe saw that dull jacket" — he glanced toward Tess's jacket — "and thought it was a buck in shadow."

"Hey, I put on this red scarf."

Looking at me, he said, "That gray jacket's no better. A little bit of color's not enough. You two ought to be wearing fluorescent orange vests this time of year if you're doing any walking in the woods. Just common sense."

Few people tower over me; this man treated me like a child. I consider myself street-smart, but apparently I'm not woods-smart. Even so, if he patted me on my head he was going to lose his arm. He caught the look in my eye and took a step back.

It was the last day of the firearms season for deer hunting anyway, he said, to be followed by two weeks of archery season. Archers were usually a safer sort, less likely to be drunk, he said.

I had just opened my mouth to chew him out royally when Tess said a quick good-bye and got us away fast.

"I don't want to make too big a scene," she defended her actions. "Like he said, if somebody really wanted us dead, we'd be dead. And I have to get along in this town."

"It's your call," I said. "I thought you said everybody accepted you by now."

"No, what I said was, *just about* everybody. Money buys a lot of acceptance. But there was a letter to the Ironwood *Globe* from the good Reverend Hudspeth after we met at the village council meeting. He said I'd be bringing in gay men for orgies and spreading AIDS to all the womenfolk."

My head jerked.

"I wrote back and pointed out that lesbians must be God's chosen people because we had the lowest rate for AIDS of any sexually active group there was, and he could look at the statistics and see heterosexual men were the ones who did the raping."

I had to laugh at the idea of lesbians requiring

gay men for sex orgies. It reminded me of the time I came out to a new clothing store owner on Hyperion. I told him I owned a lesbian bar. "What do you do in the bar?" he asked. Well, we danced, and drank, and got to know each other, I told him. He kept asking where I got the men from, and I kept asking what men he had in mind. He finally said that we must bring in men for the dancing. He absolutely could not fathom that women could *dance* together, though he seemed to understand we slept together. If he'd dared, he undoubtedly would have eventually asked what it was lesbians actually did in bed without almighty penises. With his inability to understand gay lifestyles, his business didn't last long in Silverlake.

I called Kitt to tell her about the shooting incident. She told us to take care of ourselves but agreed that it probably wasn't serious. "Remind me to wear Day-Glo when I come visit," were her cheerful last words.

We transferred Radar to the Jeep and drove to Ironwood. We needed to relax, and neither of us felt like cooking. With barely a roadsign to indicate the separation, we were over the Wisconsin state line and into the town of Hurley. " 'Known for its legendary nightlife,' " Tess said, quoting a Chamber of Commerce brochure she'd tucked in her purse.

I spotted a business downtown called "Deja Vu — A Gentleman's Club," which seemed to be a strip joint. It wasn't listed in the Chamber of Commerce brochure. Maybe not legendary enough.

" 'Hurley's Number One Hotspot' " was the Horses Corral. Tess read aloud, " 'Featuring two bars, dancing and entertainment' and 'the latest in lighting and sound!' "

Wow. It had the exact same equipment my bar had back in Silverlake, just fewer dykes to enjoy it. Only two, far as I could tell, though rural women's rough and casual clothes could be easily confused with old dyke uniforms.

Tess had a screwdriver, I had a Diet Pepsi, and then we went for dinner at the Liberty Bell Chalet. "This is the best you're going to get at a restaurant in this area," Tess warned me. I'd wanted Mexican. We got Italian. "Forget quesadillas," she said, "for the duration."

Over two excellent small pizzas — mine with anchovies — and an antipasto, we got over the incident. The sheriff was probably right. Even though the land was posted, we were stupid to have walked in the woods in muted colors.

Back at the lodge I made sure Radar couldn't get out of the kitchen again. Tess showed me around some more, starting with the woodshed, which was connected by a breezeway to the kitchen. There must have been forty linear feet of chest-high stacks of assorted hard woods, mainly sugar maple, birch and hemlock, cut into fourteen-inch lengths, along with kindling branches and stacks of newspapers.

Did I hear a faint chirping, scurrying sound?

"Field mice." Tess shrugged. "They're all over the place. Woodpiles are notorious for mice. The living room furniture was full of chewed spots and mouse turds, which is why I had it pitched. I'm going to have to start setting traps." She wrinkled her nose.

The prospect didn't thrill me. Being the butch,

not to mention the employee, guess who was probably going to be the one setting and emptying those traps?

"If we were going to stay here through the winter I'd get cats. Or you could bring that kitten of yours when she gets well. We need a good mouser. But not with us coming and going. Cats generally don't like traveling."

For extra bedtime warmth, we each made a small fire in our rooms. The furnace wasn't that great in keeping every room toasty. Tess said that by the time the ashes cooled we'd be fast asleep under quilts and blankets. She didn't say what we were supposed to do about leaving those blankets behind in the morning.

I locked my door to keep Radar in my room. During her evening walk she'd kept straining against the leash almost beyond my ability to hold her. She'd left her brains in L.A. This was not working out.

Tess knocked and came in one more time to loan me a thick terry floor-length wrap-around robe, flannel pajamas and pile-lined slippers to tide me over until the fire's heat permeated the room. She'd also made two hot chocolates using the microwave in her room.

"We Yoopers have this down to a science, conserving energy and heat at the same time we don't have to suffer," she said, laughing.

"You're hardly a Yooper after one summer and fall," I said. "After all, you're the one who put on a denim jacket to go out walking in the woods during deer-hunting season."

"Touché. But I'm learning. I can say 'You betcha,' and end every sentence with 'eh?' with the best of them. My yesses will turn to 'yahs' soon enough."

She dropped into a thickened dialect that sounded more like the "Saturday Night Live" crew imitating Chicago Bears fans. I hadn't noticed any difference in the way people talked at the restaurant or stores.

"It's a kind of self-mockery thing, making fun of the region's ethnic roots," she said. "You're right, people don't talk that way much around here, just when they're telling Yooper jokes. But you will hear 'eh?' at the end of a lot of sentences. Probably the Canadian influence. I'll be talking like a native in a few days."

Tess warmed her hands near the blue-streaked yellow flames. "The hardest thing for me about adjusting to the U.P. was letting go and actually burning wood. Firewood is so expensive in L.A., and we think of trees as endangered species. In reality, with just the naturally occurring deadwood from these thousand acres, we could keep fireplaces going in every cabin and room every cool night of the year and not make a dent in the woodpile."

She stoked my fireplace as she talked. We were admiring each other's efforts like Girl Scouts who had just earned our camping badges, reluctant to go to bed yet.

"I had a crew come in here and cut up the deadwood last spring, but the forest needs it again," Tess said. "I could sell off enough firewood for half of the county, except that everybody already has their own firewood."

She tucked a half-burnt log into the flames.

"We have such an abundance here. When L.A. is going through a drought, a lot of your politicians keep looking wistfully at the Great Lakes, trying to figure out how to build another pipeline. And people

109

from L.A. and Chicago are buying up Lake Superior coastline as fast as it goes on the market, at outlandish prices." We pondered the world's problems and went to sleep.

Overnight it snowed. A foot-deep snow that Tess at first insisted was premature, then admitted was overdue. "At least you got to see the place yesterday before the ground got covered. This area probably won't see earth again till May."

Apparently the snow had stopped and the snow removal service had come through once, but then the snow had started again. I cleared the porch entryway with a snow shovel from the woodshed.

"Come on, Radar, you're in for a treat," I said, snapping on her chain leash and wrapping it twice around my forearm in case she tried to struggle free again. But she didn't want to go out. She growled at the white flakes and snapped at them like they were gnats.

When I tugged her off the porch she erupted into a frenzy and promptly fell into a snow drift over her head. She yelped like a hyena and writhed deeper into the show, a study in pure terror. On her back, her legs thrashed.

She scrambled out, puzzled, shaking, and tumbled back to the lodge front door, an emotional wreck. She picked up each paw and shook off the snow, licking at her fur. If a dog could cry, we'd be drowning.

"What's the matter, Radar?" I tried to comfort her. She acted like she was on fire, lunging at each snowflake like a flame.

"Maybe she's sick," Tess said. Together we held

down the ninety-pound dog and looked for any sign of something wrong, an injury from yesterday maybe, desperate to soothe the shepherd.

Radar broke free and shook her whole body, trying to get the ice out of her coat, then rolled on the floor as if she were ablaze. She bit at her feet, snapping at the cold particles between her toes. The dog was a nervous wreck. She wouldn't go out again.

All day long we battled, me pulling at her by her leash, Tess pushing at her rear, trying to get her out the door. She peed on the doorway but wouldn't step outside. I yelled at her and felt totally frustrated.

"She's never acted like this before," I apologized as I cleaned the doorway with paper towels and Lysol.

Radar urinated at the doorstep again that day and still wouldn't budge into the snowy outdoors. Then she dumped in a corner of my bedroom.

"Did you ever hear of a dog that hated snow this much?" I asked the four walls.

After two days of this, I finally called Anne. She had no explanation either. "Why don't you send her back here?" Anne said.

"You'd take care of her?"

"Always room for another critter, you know that. I can't stand to think of her suffering that way. After all, I'm the one who found her for you. I love her too."

I couldn't bear to watch Radar cower. And she could still escape and run deer, and I didn't want to face the possibility of losing her to a bullet from a wildlife agent and facing a huge fine.

Reluctantly I agreed.

She assured me Flirt was doing great. "She sleeps on your old pillow next to me on the waterbed."

My cheeks burned. I didn't want to even think about that image. Was Anne deliberately rubbing it in? I could still hear her telling me it was all over, she could never take me back. She'd never said anything to the contrary since then. I must be looking for nonexistent hidden meanings, I told myself. Of course the prized new kitten would get the best bed in the house.

I could make myself crazy wondering if there was still some hope of recapturing something that was no longer in evidence. And I was committed to Hayley — wasn't I? Yes, I was. I hadn't given her enough time to recover, that's all. I wasn't going to assume it was over until I heard it from her. Or until I called at Christmas, whichever came first.

"Stop it, Laney," H.P. said. "Serenity *now!*" And I missed whatever Anne was saying. She repeated her question about the nearest airport.

We made arrangements to ship Radar from the Duluth airport, which had a direct flight to Burbank that Anne could meet. At most, Radar would be in a cage for seven or eight hours. I didn't want to risk sending her off from the small Ironwood airport that only had commuter flights to Chicago and Minneapolis, not knowing how long she'd be between flights, probably without heat.

"We'll do some shopping while we're in Duluth, get you some more warm clothes," Tess promised. A new wardrobe was hardly going to make me feel better.

Radar give me a worried kiss good-bye through

the air holes in the pet carrier. "Good-bye, you good, good dog," I said, trying not to cry. "I'll see you soon. Promise."

And now my dog was out of my life for two or three weeks, maybe more. My protector, my companion, my friend. I couldn't quite feel safe without her around. As we walked back to the Jeep through the beginnings of a new snowfall in Duluth, I said so.

"Despite the shots in the woods, Beer Barrel is a very safe place," Tess countered. "The crime rate is almost zilch, except for drunk driving and a few thefts at the summer cottages that are left vacant during the winter. Mainly it's teenagers looking for mischief." The sheriff had said something similar.

"Real comforting," I said. "Put it on my tombstone if I get shot by some hunter: 'Beer Barrel is a very safe place.' "

Tess hit me with a snowball. The fight was on.

CHAPTER ELEVEN

Rudy was back when we returned, loading cardboard boxes and luggage into his navy Suburban. I wouldn't have believed he was eighty. He seemed as spry and wiry as a fifty-year-old in top form. Hey, *I'm* fifty, I realized. He'd probably beat me on my morning walks.

He was shorter than me, but our wavy silver hair and gray-blue eyes matched. I hoped I didn't have the suspicious, angry, cold attitude that he carried as easily as the packages.

Then I noticed how he favored his right leg, as if his hip hurt him with every step. Shades of things to come; I sometimes felt a twinge in my hip at night. And I spotted the way he camouflaged his frequent stops to catch his breath, pretending to examine the tape on the edges of the boxes, taking time over a close look at a pit in the windshield. Discreetly he rubbed the small of his back through his blue nylon parka. This was a man in pain who would never admit it. At first glance no one would know. Why had he kept on working? After all these years he probably felt he owned the place.

"We missed you the past couple of days," Tess said. "This is Laney Samms. She's here to help with some planning and paperwork. Laney, Rudy Braun."

Without looking at us, he gave a final shove to a blue Samsonite suitcase. "I quit," he said.

Tess looked at me in delight, then masked her expression. "I'm sorry to hear that," she said. "What made you decide to leave?"

At first I thought he wouldn't answer. Finally he said, "My daughter found a senior citizens apartment near her, and she says I shouldn't be working anymore. Can't say no to the womenfolk, eh? Hate to leave you in the lurch."

"It's all right, Rudy," Tess said. "We'll manage."

"Ask him about the botched lake dredging," I murmured.

"Oh . . . that's okay. I can handle it. Sorry to see you go, Rudy. When will you be out?"

Here's your hat, what's your hurry?

"Gone now. If you find anything I left, throw it away. Or if it looks valuable, send it care of my daughter's, eh? You've got her address."

He seemed as anxious to get away from us as we were to have him gone.

Tess checked out his room afterward. "Clean as a whistle. Smells like a man, though." We opened the window even though it was freezing outside. And snowing. Again. I wrinkled my nose.

"Get used to it," Tess said.

I checked the fax basket and e-mail for any messages from Kitt. None. I called her and tried to pin her down on a date that she'd be here.

"If I didn't know better, I'd think you were avoiding the trip," I said. "What I really need right now are the names of some lesbian interior decorators somewhere nearby."

"Don't be ridiculous. I said I'd be out in two weeks and I'll be out. Things are really hectic here, that's all. I'll make arrangements soon, don't worry. I'll fax you the names you need."

An hour later the fax whirred and fed out the names of two lesbian interior decorators in Minneapolis/St. Paul to get us started. The first one, Shelby Curtis, was available and eager. We made arrangements for her to come to Beer Barrel to tour the lodge the following Monday. She was going to be out of town over Thanksgiving, so she had to see us before then.

Thanksgiving already! I'd been at the lodge for three days and hadn't paid any attention to the upcoming holiday. Time was flying.

That week I attacked my work list. First I went to the local library and checked out the newspapers, magazines and broadcasting stations serving the area. I had my national media lists but they don't always list the smaller media which can be so important in

116

gaining community support. I had two tasks: build awareness of the music festival itself, once we had some firm dates and acts; and promote Tess and her business to the Ironwood residents so that they would have a favorable image and understanding of what she was doing.

The editor of the Ironwood *Globe* referred me to the reporter he called his Brenda Starr wanna-be. "Hi, hot shot," he said when she came into his office to meet me. "Wanda Krakabowski, meet Laney Samms." Only the slightest tightening of Wanda's body language indicated she detested the patronizing. She was slender and had black straight hair that fell to her hips, held back from her face with a paisley headband. Her intense brown eyes and glowing olive complexion — unusual, given her last name — gave a hint of her determination and ambition.

When we got back to her desk I gave her a sympathetic smile and she let out a growl, glaring back in her editor's direction. "I'm up for the next opening at the *Marquette Mining Journal*," she said. "It's the biggest daily in the U.P. From there I want to get the hell out of Dodge. But no big paper's going to hire me from a weekly. This was the only job I could get — journalism is a flooded field. It's worse than law school."

I'd watched a Miss America pageant one night when I was bored and had noticed how many beautiful young women were majoring in communications and wanted to anchor the national news some day. So many women, so few slots. Wanda was as likely as anyone to make it to the top, however.

She proved understanding of the concept of a

women's music festival, and she filled me in on community leaders and organizations I should contact. In return I gave her enough information to run a short feature on the lodge and on Tess, which she would supplement with a phone interview with Tess herself later that day. I scheduled visits with several groups and leaders Wanda had suggested and found she'd been right about their helpfulness. There was a women's business organization in Ironwood which seemed to include every thinking female in the county, most of them well-placed to be of help later.

Though they were more than a hundred miles away, I decided to pay a visit to Marquette and Escanaba where Tess said there were a few open gays and lesbians. At Sweet Violets bookstore in Marquette I gained more information about the gay and lesbian community in the U.P. and added to my mailing lists. I made dozens of phone calls to local leaders and to vendors, checking out dates and availabilities. The Fourth of July weekend seemed the best, though there were the inevitable conflicting schedules. Kitt wanted to contact the performers herself, and she too was running into roadblocks with conflicting events scheduled long before ours.

Not enough time, I kept hearing the nagging voice inside tell me. And somehow the concept of one big music festival in July seemed a terrible waste of the facility. We couldn't even start to get the grounds in shape for campers until late spring. Would we need an Environmental Protection Agency permit? Or the Department of Natural Resources approval? More details to check out.

Every time I went past the thirty smaller log cabins with their eight bunk beds each, an incipient idea started to poke its way into my consciousness. I kept thinking of the cabins the writers stayed at in *Claire of the Moon*.

Finally I had the concept. The lodge could become a year-round arts center, with up to thirty individual lesbian artists and musicians receiving grants to live in the cabins for free to finish their works in progress. The only stipulation would be that they would have to provide some sort of entertainment or workshops for visitors who would come all summer long! Maybe spring and fall too, and maybe even winter performances combined with winter sports activities in the area. Tess could offer the equivalent of a major liberal arts campus just for lesbians!

"You're brilliant!" Tess cried out at my plan, rushing in with ideas of her own as I talked. "This is a way I can help the lesbian community better than anything I've ever dreamed! This is far better than an annual music festival."

Kitt said she liked the idea in theory but to hold off on any definite arrangements until she got there to see the layout for herself. She was having a hard time visualizing how this arts center would function, now that our ideas were sprouting in all directions with all sorts of possibilities evolving every day.

"Better hurry, because we're bound to get a really big snowstorm any day now," Tess warned. "You don't want to be socked in at the airport. You can still see the lay of the land around here between snow drifts, but not for long." Kitt promised to do her best.

Tess and Kitt seemed to be spending a lot of time on the phone each night, for which I was glad. I told Tess to think of ways she'd like to choose the winning artists who would get to live at the lodge. Should she set up her own foundation just to receive grant applications? Should we get the lawyers and accountants involved now? And who would she like to have among the judges?

We decided that we didn't need to select all thirty women immediately, though some artists could certainly be chosen by spring. They could alternate their weekend performances with workshops for women who might want to stay at the lodge all week long. Those who didn't perform could teach classes and seminars. The ideas kept flying, one on top of another, relayed to L.A. via e-mail, while Kitt kept saying, "Wait! Slow down! I'll get there as soon as I can." It was hard to contain ourselves.

I remembered a classmate in high school who had been selected to attend Interlochen, an arts center near Traverse City which hosted high school students for intensive summer school sessions and which held both student and professional concerts and art shows in the summer.

We took a quick trip down to Interlochen and met with the administrators to gather more ideas. They gave us the names of some attorneys and CPAs who were familiar with their structure, and Kitt agreed that these would be the best people to hire to help Tess. I started pressing Tess to get her to commit to a business plan, even to come up with a business objective, a one-sentence summary of her goal for the business, and to think about how much money she wanted to commit to it.

She did agree that the nonprofit foundation route that Interlochen used seemed best. The lawyers advised that she could turn over the remodeled facility to the foundation and serve on its board of directors to retain some control. She would divert two million dollars a year tax-free this way to her projects. If the foundation ever disbanded or the lodge was no longer needed, the property would revert to Tess or her heirs, the lawyers said.

She rolled her eyes at those words — "My God, don't make me have to think about heirs."

"It's an in-joke kind of thing," I explained to the consultants. "By the way, Tess, you do have a will, don't you?" The lawyers also sat her down to think about that aspect of the business plan.

Some tasks were no brainers. Before Shelby Curtis arrived, Tess and I went through the cabins and outbuildings again and noted the masculine artifacts that would likely offend a city lesbian's sensibilities. Carved wood mallards remained, stuffed bass landed in a box to be donated to St. Vincent de Paul thrift shop in Ironwood.

Tess's main enjoyment was cooking scrumptious meals each night. I missed slipping leftovers to Radar. Anne called to say that the lab tests reported nothing wrong with Radar physically. The dog had reverted to normal the moment she'd hit Anne's back yard. Anne got excited when I told her of my ideas for an ongoing arts center that would support dozens of lesbian artists. "Think of the exchanges of ideas that will happen when you get all those creative women together!" Anne exclaimed. "Have I told you lately that you're brilliant?" I was glad she couldn't see my flaming cheeks.

When the interior decorator arrived, with an assistant who looked like she belonged in high school, she brought catalogs of women's arts and crafts.

Shelby told us that she unwound at the National Women's Music Festival in Indiana each June, and she knew exactly what we needed. I could picture her shedding her houndstooth wool blazer and pleated trousers at a Topp Twins concert, though the campus setting wasn't conducive to topless. Andi, her assistant, was in jeans and a sweatshirt and did the dirty work of measuring rooms and photographing every angle.

"Women are going to love this place," Shelby kept saying as she explored the lodge. She kept pushing her dark pageboy out of her face with her left hand and adjusting her tortoise shell glasses on her nose with the same motion.

She recommended inexpensive and sturdy art pieces. Tess argued for really fine things. "I can afford it," she insisted. "Besides, women take care of things better."

"Don't idealize the community," I responded. "You get a bunch of rowdy dykes together and they're just as likely to cause havoc as the past inhabitants of these cabins." Shelby agreed with me.

The day flew. While Andi took measurements and Polaroids, Tess and I examined catalogs with Shelby. We chose hefty wood block style furniture with varying colors of plaids and prints.

"We'd like to have the architectural plans for the building too," Shelby said. "Do you have them, or can you get them for us? That way, we'll know where the structural walls are that bear most of the building's weight, where the lighting conduits are, that sort of thing."

I went down to the county offices and was told

the lodge's plans couldn't be found. But an elderly employee remembered the name of the architect, long since dead. "He used the same basic plan for a lot of the big fancy hunting lodges around this country," the man, George Schiller, told me. "They were all the rage, you know."

I nodded. "I heard that Henry Ford and a lot of other rich people built lodges in the U.P."

"Not just Michigan. I seem to remember that one of the lodges that this same architect built with the same plans was near Chicago somewheres. They hold meetings there now. I remember, the Lake Michigan Conference Center. I don't remember exactly where it was, but maybe you can find it from that much. They should have the plans, maybe."

A few calls to directory information for the area codes in Illinois and I tracked down the Lake Michigan Conference Center and ordered a copy of their plans to be sent to Shelby and another to Tess. The Center's general manager didn't know about the shared blueprints but noted that a famous hotel designer, John Portman, had used his same design on several recently built hotels. "A big hotel in Atlanta and one in Detroit each have four round towers, mostly tinted glass, seventy stories high," he said. "They have flashy glass elevators that climb up the outsides of the towers and a big open garden atrium in the center. I think there's a similar hotel in Los Angeles, though not as tall."

I nodded. "The Bonaventure. And the one in Atlanta is in the Peachtree Center, and the Detroit one is in the Renaissance Center. I remember reading about Portman's brand new concept when the

Bonaventure opened. So it wasn't such a new idea after all, then. Thanks a lot for helping us out." One more item to cross off of my to-do list.

On Thanksgiving Tess made a wonderful traditional dinner. Feeling silly, I called Anne and asked her to put the phone against Radar's ear. Radar barked in delight as I told her about all the leftovers that she could have had if she'd shaped up.

"Don't worry, she got some of mine," Anne said. "Flirt too." I missed L.A.

Almost every day more snow fell. The snow removal service swiftly followed to clear our driveways and the paths to the outbuildings. I relearned to apply brakes gently, to steer in the direction of a skid, and to keep a small shovel, tire chains, blankets, flashlights, and a bag of kitty litter in the back of the Jeep to provide traction when I got stuck.

Tess got advice on what else needed to be done for the winter. One last delivery topped off the fuel oil tanks. Plenty of firewood overflowed the stacks. A sizeable pile was brought inside at the truck delivery area, for those days when it would be impossible to even make it to the woodshed.

Tess and I scavenged the gigantic pantry. We found a few boxes and cans that hadn't been thrown out in 1989 and tossed them in the garbage.

"I hate to throw away food," Tess said. "It must be how our generation was raised. Remember being told to eat everything on your plate because of starving children in China?"

She patted her comfortable belly. "So I did. My getting fat didn't help anyone in China, far as I can tell."

I appreciated her frank talk about weight and size, and her own self-acceptance. I wondered if my immediate dismissal of her as "not my type" was my own prejudice. I'd think about that some other time.

When we were in the gas station's convenience store one day buying milk, Tess started talking aloud about maybe spending the winter. "I can't possibly get everything done by mid-December the way I'd hoped."

Thal Swanson seemed to be straining to hear our words. "You'll never make it through January alive," he grunted at Tess as he made change for her purchase. "You girls oughta be out of there right now." There was an urgency to his voice.

"Why Thal, I didn't know you cared about our well-being," Tess chuckled.

"You ought to get yourselves back to California right now. Today!" His warning was guttural, and he kept shifting his eyes as if worried some unseen person in the empty store would overhear his words.

Tess and I looked at each other. "Sorry, we're staying," she said. I couldn't recognize the expression on his face. He was valiantly trying to control some emotion.

Outside, Tess and I wondered aloud what he had meant. "He's probably missing Rita even more as the nights get longer and colder," Tess decided. I agreed. "By the way, what do you think about having some big professional acts perform along with the women who are getting the grants?" she said. "Or what about getting some high school students up here like Interlochen? Do you think we can give college credits? How do you get academic certification?" She was off and running in a thousand directions at once.

I hoped she'd forget half her ideas until we were solid with the basics. And somehow I couldn't imagine our being allowed to host high school students at a lesbian camp for school credit. Maybe college, through some liberal school like Antioch. We'd talk about it later.

On my Toshiba notebook, I played around with rough sketches of logos and advertising designs in QuarkXPress, though a graphics pro would do the final work. Kitt and I had both been eyeing the new Pentium notebooks in the seven-thousand-dollar range, but we agreed that our 486 models did everything we needed them to do. It seems to be men who want new bells and whistles for the sake of showing off, whether they actually need the new capabilities or not. "More power," as Tim Allen would grunt.

Sometimes I wish I'd gotten started on Macintosh, which retains the lead in graphics capabilities, but once entrenched in IBM clones, it's hard to switch. Yes, I know, the new wonder software allows you to switch back and forth between them, but that requires a few extra steps, and I'm not sure it's worth it. Kitt had an office suite package which included a spreadsheet, with which I tried to cajole Tess. "It's easy, just plug in a guesstimate here . . ." But she was having none of it.

I needed to be arranging for advertising already for some of the women's publications with long lead times, but nothing was firm. Oh yeah, I could do an ad: "Hey women, we're gonna have something grand out here next summer, only we don't know what or when or how much it's gonna cost or any other details, but be here and be queer!" We didn't even have a new name for the joint yet. No self-respecting dyke would spend money at the Tessel Hunting and Fishing Lodge. Although a few successful L.A. lesbian events have been held at the Sportsmen's Lodge in Sherman Oaks.

I tried to get a realistic picture of Tess's financial situation. The figures amazed me. If the lodge was a bottomless money pit, so was her income — just the interest more than covered everything she'd spent so far. The Tessel account seemed to single-handedly support a major Grosse Pointe bank and a CPA firm, as well as the attorneys we'd visited.

"Tess never seemed interested in details," one accountant told me. "I'm glad somebody's paying attention to the reports we send out." His answers to my questions reassured me that Tess really didn't have to worry about running out of money. But I still felt bound to get Tess to agree to a business plan and to a budget, at least for some of the ideas we seemed sure of. She wasn't giving the Interlochen consultants any more cooperation than she was me, and they were costing her a hell of a lot more.

"What do I need a budget for?" Tess kept telling all of us. "I've got plenty of money. It doesn't matter what anything costs."

"You still need a business plan, with some sort of guidelines for spending," I insisted. "Let's get real basic. How will you know you're a success if you don't put down your definition of what being a success means?" She threw up her hands at me.

The consultants from Interlochen finally got hardnosed with her. She couldn't apply for nonprofit tax status without goals, plans, budgets and projections. She sighed and got to work, but it was like putting lipstick on a butch. I left another message for Kitt to get here quick.

Finally I got her on the phone. " 'Soon' isn't a good enough answer," I pushed her. "You can't believe all we've accomplished in a couple of weeks, working our tails off, but it's already December. December three, to be exact. We're going to be socked in any day now."

Silence.

"Hey, you sent me here. I'm handling it. Kitt, I tell you, I need you here. I don't feel I can go any further without you seeing the place and agreeing with what I've come up with so far. I think I've got a good working plan drawn up, and it flies with the CPA and lawyer, but then Tess goes off in another direction on us. She finally saw the need for a budget and business plan but it's not happening."

"All right, all right. She's been calling me to come up there too."

"I bet you take her calls."

"You're damned right. Persistent, damn her. I admire that in a client. She's a pretty interesting person, isn't she?"

"Come on, I want an ETA."

"Okay already. I'm checking my calendar. Maybe a vacation is a good thing. I need to get away. You can't believe the pressure I'm under around here. Maybe Tess has the right idea, find some idyllic little out-of-the-way spot of heaven and work from there. I'm ready for something new. Are there any fall colors left?"

"Sure, under half a foot of snow."

"I guess. Okay, here's some time I can reschedule. December eight, all right?"

We made the arrangements.

And then on December four, a Saturday, we heard on the radio that the first real snowstorm was due overnight. I worried that the snow wouldn't be cleared enough to pick up Kitt at Ironwood on the eighth.

"You've seen the plows in action. They can handle it," Tess kept reassuring me.

We and everyone else for miles around drove into the Union 76 convenience store to pick up last-minute needs. Tess and I were out of skim milk and diet Pepsi, our usual shopping list items for the store. For major outlays we drove to the super-markets in Ironwood.

We nodded greetings to Joe Underwood, whose chubby face and three chins looked as incongruous as ever contrasted with his skinny legs. He tried to wrap the Ironwood *Globe* around the package of Depends he was buying. Was it for him or his wife, I wondered. Not that it mattered — those wonderful older movie queens hawking the stuff on TV said it would happen to all of us sooner or later. Idly I noted to myself that it had been a long time since I'd needed any Tampax. Oh well. I wasn't going to miss having periods.

Tess pointed out the Reverend Mark Hudspeth, wearing a snagged polyester houndstooth sports jacket and shiny-kneed black pants under his camouflage-painted parka. In his arms were two packages each of bacon and eggs. He gave a curt acknowledgment of Tess's introduction. I tried my best to look like someone who'd bring in gay men for an orgy.

"I hear you're staying a few more weeks," he questioned Tess, his eyes burning at her.

"That's right," she said with a hint of defiance in her voice. "And maybe all winter."

"Hah! You'll be sorry," the minister said.

I recognized the Lucille Ball tilt to Tess's head as she formulated some smart-ass response, and I took her by the arm and led her to the magazine rack to calm down. Hudspeth shot looks of hate at us and at the ominous sky as he left.

Thal Swanson gave up on trying to pump gas and wait on people simultaneously. People pumped for themselves and survived. I decided the man offered full service only because he was bored to death sitting around inside waiting for customers. He probably had some satisfying conversations with his other customers while he pumped their gas and cleaned their windshields. Probably we were the only ones to get the silent treatment.

Wearing the same greasy brown insulated jumpsuit he'd had on before, he kept his eyes focused on the cash register when the line brought us to the check out counter. I wondered if he'd wash the suit anytime before spring.

"Be sure and have Karl hit our place with his snowplow as soon as he can," Tess said. "You'll talk to him tonight, right?" To me she said, "They live across from each other."

Thal grunted. Customers crowded the counter.

"And have him cut some snowmobile trails too, will you? I want to show Laney how to use a snowmobile tomorrow! It should be a perfect day for it. I can't wait."

Another grunt. Groans from others in line.

"I'll take that as a yes," Tess said. "Glad to see business is so good for you, Thal. Have a great night weathering the storm." The lights flickered inside the store while the gray skies outside grew distinctly darker.

Thal gave Tess her change, while dozens of local denizens moved up one place in line. "You don't know what you're in for," he muttered almost inaudibly.

Tess grinned back at him. "We're ready."

"What are you so happy about?" Underwood said from his position at the end of the line, his chins wattling. "You've never seen a real storm. You'll wish you'd gone back to California."

Other old-timers nodded. The general agreement seemed to be that we were all in the valley of the doomed. Only Tess seemed happy about the coming storm.

I wondered yet another time what I had gotten myself into. What was the December temperature in Tahiti?

CHAPTER TWELVE

I awoke in the morning to a world that even sounded different. Muffled, heavy, quiet. The throaty rumble of the oil furnace kicked on at that moment, and I could see light through the frosted window, reassuring signs that I hadn't been buried alive. But when I scraped a circle of ice off the inside of my second-story window I wasn't so sure.

I could see ground below, but it was a good two feet nearer to me than yesterday. I could feel the earth coming up closer and closer. My breath felt heavy, my energy stifled. We were going to be stuck inside this log cabin structure for weeks, months. Forever. I'm not a claustrophobic, but this panic must be what they suffer.

Another part of my brain interjected: a few moments snowed in and this is how I feel? What would I be like in another month?

"Good morning!" Tess's voice trilled through the door. "I've got blueberry pancakes ready! It's beautiful out, have you looked?"

Was she in a different time zone? Another planet?

"It's horrible," I said. The snow outside seemed to be rising higher and higher, like floodwaters, even though only a few flakes were falling.

"Good, you're up. Decent?" She waltzed into my room and joined me at the window. She smelled of maple syrup and sausage. Flour dusted her navy University of Michigan sweatshirt and navy sweatpants. She had on Garfield fuzzy slippers. I shivered in my borrowed flannel PJs and dug my muk-luks out from under the bed. Where was that thick robe she'd gotten me in Duluth, along with all the other winter clothes? I had a feeling I'd use the entire wardrobe today.

"Remember 'The Shining'? I expect any minute now Jack Nicholson will jump out from behind a snowdrift with an axe," I said. "It's eerie. Horrible!"

"You can think of it that way," she said, waving a browned sausage under my nose. "Or you can remember that we're here for a while longer and we might as well make the best of it. Try again."

"You sound like my smart-ass Higher Power," I grumbled. I narrowed my eyes and thought Currier & Ives greeting cards. Over the river and through the snow, to Grandmother's house we go, tra la. At least downstairs to the kitchen. Suddenly I was starved. I followed the sausage.

"Okay, so it is pretty," I admitted once I was full of carbohydrates, proteins and too much fat. I hadn't taken my morning walk for a few days and felt it. "How the hell do we get out of here?"

"The snowplow's already been here," she said. "Though we've got a fresh sprinkling starting again. I told you Karl always does my place first. I gave him a big bonus last Christmas. He made snowmobile paths too — this is the weather for it. Ready to learn how to ride a snowmobile? Dress warmly."

I had every intention of doing just that. Layering is the magic word for braving cold weather. I put on the white thermal long-sleeved undershirt and leggings set that Tess had insisted upon, followed by a flannel shirt-jacket and flannel-lined jeans. Thin nylon socks next to the skin are supposed to pull moisture from the skin, then wool hunting socks add insulation before pulling on waterproof boots.

At the kitchen door, which was closest to the garage, we put on more layers: one-piece quilted snowmobile jumpsuits over everything, with fur-lined gloves and wool ski masks, topped with crash helmets in colors to match the jumpsuits. Mine was black with blue pinstriping down the arms, hers a vivid yellow with blocks of red and orange.

Our goggles had gray lenses for sun, with a flip-down set of yellow lenses, "for flat afternoon sun and white-outs," Tess said. She'd gotten us outfitted with all sorts of accessories at a Duluth sporting goods emporium.

"We're supposed to be able to move?" I said. "Ma, I have to go to the bathroom."

"Hush up, we're going to have fun."

"Only if you insist."

Outside I was thankful for every layer. The thermometer outside the kitchen read seven degrees. Fahrenheit, not Centigrade. The light snow finally stopped, and the sky was a miraculous blue, after the typical Michigan winter overcast. I made the mistake of breathing deeply through my mouth, just once. My chest hurt for long minutes afterward.

We followed the plowed paths to the garage, where a dozen snowmobiles were parked. "Karl checked them all out last month, and they're ready to go," Tess said. "You pick one by weight — the flotation factor." The heavier your weight, the larger surface area of the track you need to float on the snow with, she explained. "Rule of thumb: pick one that weighs about twice as much as you do." She pointed to some in the three-hundred-pound range for me and took a bigger one for herself.

For some reason, I didn't feel comfortable being on a smaller snowmobile than Tess's — was that the butch in me? The little ones looked rinky-dink, and I didn't trust them. So I took one like hers: four hundred and fifty pounds, forty horsepower. I almost did a Tim Allen grunt.

"You won't have the control you want on that machine," Tess said.

I wouldn't budge.

"It's your funeral," she said. "You're going to have to work harder at making your turns."

I nodded, unmoving. I liked this one. On what grounds, I had no idea. Maybe because it was black with blue accents, like my suit. "I insist."

"All right then, I guess. It's not that much

heavier, maybe you'll be okay." She stared at my chosen Ski-Doo, then shrugged. "Anyway, they're all gassed up, and they've got their emergency packs ready," Tess said. "First thing you do is check out the kit to make sure it's complete."

Under the seat in my storage compartment, I found tools, rope, a small first aid kit, waterproofed coated matches. Extra gloves, socks, ski mask and goggles. An aluminum space blanket, compass, county terrain map, flashlight, Swiss Army knife, signaling mirror, flares, compass, candles. Granola bars. Spare drive belt, spark plugs, drive chain, starting rope. The kit made me feel oh, so secure. I climbed on board.

Tess showed me how to work the controls. "Squeeze the throttle lever below the right handgrip for the gas," she said. "Too much throttle and you'll do a wheelie. Speed up with your thumb if you hit soft snow to avoid getting bogged down. Slow down on ice to give you more control. Steer in the direction of the skid."

My mind boggled.

Tess wasn't through. "If your thumb slips off, the throttle goes to idle and you stop — that's a safety feature. Count on getting snowmobiler's thumb — your thumb will go numb from having to exert continuous pressure."

I couldn't wait.

"For regular braking, the brake lever is above the left handgrip. The harder you squeeze, the faster you stop — but don't count on jackknife stops. You can end up in a ditch."

Can and probably will, I thought to myself.

"If you're in trouble and don't know what to do,

bail out, the softest way you can," she said. "Pick a snowbank and let yourself land in it."

That I could probably do too.

"Okay, time to get going. There's an electric start using a key in the ignition switch, but there's also a backup manual start with a rope. Let the engine idle a few minutes to warm up."

The Ski-Doo sounded like a jackhammer, despite improved exhaust and noise control systems she said were developed in recent years.

"Anybody up here who doesn't own a snowmobile hates everyone who does, especially tourists who take shortcuts through front yards and don't stick to the maintained trails. The trails generally follow abandoned railroad lines. But we've got plenty of trails right here."

I thought there was enough trail in the parking lot. We practiced driving in circles. Turning the handlebars didn't guarantee a turn, I found. I had to "hike out."

"Lean into the opposite direction from which you're turning, so that your weight gives an extra bite to the edge of the track," Tess explained. "For a right turn, keep your left knee on the seat and shift your weight onto your right foot on the running board. That way you take any jolts in your legs. Less tiring."

"This is hard work!" I said, zigzagging around her and yelling to be heard.

"You don't just sit back in a snowmobile," she yelled back. "Snowmobilers tend to wear out the seats of their pants, sliding back and forth for control."

"And I was worried how I was going to keep in shape. Especially with sausage and pancakes for breakfast."

"Don't worry, you're going to use every calorie."

Slowly we took off on a trail away from the lodge. On a slight hill Tess showed me how to go up in a Zee pattern, crossing side to side like sailboat tacking, leaning into the hill for traction.

The brilliant blue sky belied the cold. If I let myself admit it, the day was totally gorgeous. Remember k.d. lang on that snowmobile, I kept telling myself, trying not to breathe through my mouth. My breaths left mushroom clouds in front of my face.

I shifted my rear on the smooth seat and felt the machine below me respond to my whims. Not exactly a vibrator, but it could be close, if I let myself get into the mood.

Not yet — I dodged a hanging branch and careened into a snowbank. Tess's laugh covered my embarrassment. We hauled my Ski-Doo out of the snow, exerting plenty of those sausage and pancake calories in the process.

"You're doing fine," she said. "Isn't it fun? Don't you wish you'd picked a smaller machine?"

H.P., get me through this.

CHAPTER THIRTEEN

We followed the trails in and out of the property and I had to admit that I was indeed having fun, though I didn't say so aloud. I adjusted my goggles to yellow when the sun hit its apex and the shadows disappeared. Like a pro I shifted my tail back and forth on the seat at every turn.

My thumb was appropriately numb, my chest hurt from the unavoidable breaths through the mouth, my cheeks burned through the ski mask, but I was having fun. Oh yes I was.

We were out of sight of the main lodge. Tess took

a sharp turn to the left, following the plowed and groomed trail. I lagged behind a hundred feet, unable to keep up with her pace.

She looked back at me, laughed and waved.

The ground broke into six-foot chunks under her Arctic Cat. The snowmobile made a tremendous splash as it sank between the chunks.

Tess's scream ended with a gurgle.

Stunned, I lost control. My snowmobile plowed into a drift.

I leaped free and ran toward Tess, taking a shortcut across the snow rather than the trail, each foot sinking two feet in the soft snow which caught me at the knees like lassos. About ten feet from where Tess had disappeared, I felt a change in the ground under the snow. It was harder, like ice underfoot. We must be over the lake. That couldn't be right.

I stopped: the ice could crack more and pitch me into the water too. But it seemed solid underfoot. And Tess's head was emerging from underwater, her thrashing arms breaking away at the slabs of ice that marked the spot her snowmobile had gone down. She tried to scream, her cries cut off as she went under again.

I had to take the chance. There was rope in the emergency kit of my snowmobile. I ran back for it and raced onto the ice, slowing as I came closer to where she'd gone under. The surface still seemed solid under my feet, no sounds of groaning or cracking, no heaving or shifting.

Until I got close to the hole where Tess had gone down. The hole was full of gray mushy ice crystals. I backed up to safety, praying that she would fight her way back up. She surfaced, gasping, and I tossed the rope her way. I lay down in the snow, spreading my legs to ease the amount of weight on any one part of the ice.

The first time she missed. She started to take off her gloves to try again and sank when her hands stopped paddling.

When she came up again she caught my second throw and grabbed on tight.

"My hands are freezing, I can't hold on," she screamed. Water from inside her safety helmet poured down over her face in a sheet as she talked. "I can't see you!"

"Hold onto that rope, whatever you do. Wrap it around your wrist and I'll pull you out. Don't worry, I'm right here. I'm going to save you."

She made as many turns as she could with the rope around her arm. She'd have a sore arm and bruises but that was not the problem now. I heaved on my end, straining with all of my might. My body slid along the snow-covered ice. For the first time in my life I wished I weighed more.

Her body wriggled its way onto a six-foot chunk of ice. It split and plunged her screaming into the icy waters once more. My heart sank along with her.

She rose to the surface and swam in a hole of ice mush surrounded by the broken floes. I kept pulling, hoping against hope that the ice under me wouldn't crack, that I'd be able to tell somehow if it was giving way, in time to scramble to safety. I kept hoping I could hold on, that I could pull hard enough, that Tess could hold on.

Her body advanced a half-foot at a time onto the next ledge of ice. This one stayed intact.

Inch by inch. She wriggled like a baby trying to crawl. Finally she was out of the water, heaving for breath, on the ice. It held. I became aware that I hadn't breathed. My gasp sent an ice storm into my lungs.

I pulled her toward me like a sled, her wet clothes catching against ridges in the ice, her skin on her hands rubbing raw, leaving patches of red in the snow. She was crying hysterically, crying that she was freezing to death. I was afraid it was true.

With the last strength in me I yanked on the rope and she slid like a giant hockey puck to my feet. I got up and grabbed her upright. "My feet! My feet hurt!" she screamed. She sat back down.

She would die in minutes from the cold. I dragged her farther from the crash site and back to where I felt cushiony grass underfoot through the snow. I couldn't move her any more without the sliding effect of the ice. She could give no help.

My snowmobile was a few feet away, still buried up to its nose in a snowbank. I left Tess for a second, while she begged, "Don't leave me!"

"It's okay, it's going to be all right," I kept saying, not at all sure my words were true. Frantically I dug in the emergency kit. There was a first aid booklet, I saw now, in the first aid kit, and I checked the index for freezing. See hypothermia.

Get the person stripped and into warm clothes, it said. Sure. One person's naked body against another's, in a sleeping bag or something similar, is the quickest way to exchange heat. Okay. I dug through the rest of the emergency supplies.

The thin aluminum folded blanket. Hurriedly I read on its plastic cover that it would provide total coverage, protection against all elements, that it would retain body heat even in the worst blizzard. I ripped off the covering and unfolded the eight-foot square. I wished I had hers as well but it was at the bottom of the lake. Why had the snowmobile path been placed over the lake? I remembered from someplace that you couldn't trust lake ice to hold a person's weight until several weeks of consistent, heavy freezing, not the off-again, on-again freezes we'd had so far.

Those thoughts would have to wait. I had to help Tess. I'd have to strip too and get my body on hers. We didn't have a sleeping bag, the aluminum blanket would have to be the "something similar." I didn't relish stripping in the cold, but it was a matter of saving Tess's life. I didn't see enough dry wood anywhere around to get a fire going; our best hope was to get back to the lodge. How many minutes would it take her to get warm enough to travel? How many minutes would it take for me to freeze to death myself?

First I had to get her soaked clothes off. The safety helmet snap was frozen; I used the emergency kit knife to get it off, like removing an overturned bucket of water that had been dumped on Tess's head. The rest of the process was like undressing a screaming, wet baby, the clothing twisting and refusing to give. I cut off much of it. Ice crystals shimmered on her shirt when I tossed it aside. Her pale skin was blue-white, puckered with goosebumps, her nipples almost navy. Tess's teeth chattered. Her voice was fading and coarse.

The kit had extra gloves, socks and a ski mask, and I struggled to dress her. Getting wet boots off of

143

a limp body is almost impossible, but I did it. On went the nylon socks and outer wool socks. I wished I had a hair dryer before putting the new ski mask on her. Her hair strands were frozen, brittle.

I didn't think it would work to strip us both naked and rely on the few millimeters thickness of the blanket to keep enough heat enclosed to warm us both. No matter how good an insulator, the blanket wasn't that thick. We'd both die.

I thought for a second and then swathed her as best I could in the aluminum space blanket and put my outer jumpsuit on her, tucking and wrapping the ends of the silver blanket around her arms and legs as I went. The jumpsuit didn't reach across her stomach and chest. I opened my flannel shirt, raised my long winter underwear, and lowered my jeans to put my nude torso against hers. My breasts were so cold they felt like marble. My stomach against hers turned to ice. I held her upright, tight against me, willing my heat to flow into her. Layers, why hadn't I put on a couple more layers? She kept moaning about her feet.

"Cheek to cheek," I told her. "Come on, we're dancing." I took off my gloves and forced my hands into hers. She alternated both sides of her face against mine, raising her ski mask for each cheek. I blew on her exposed nose to warm it. My body heat fled into her like boiling spaghetti water disappearing out a sieve. I had never been so cold in my life. I only hoped she was benefitting, that I was doing the right thing.

I was shivering myself. Shivering so severely that I thought I would fall apart. I felt as if I had no more warmth to give, maybe not enough even for myself. She seemed to be feeling better, the chattering and shivering were a little less severe, but I had to get us to safety.

"Walk with me, cheek to cheek, we're still dancing," I said, and we maneuvered over to my snowmobile. Please, have enough flotation or whatever it is to hold us both, I prayed. Thank God I wanted the heavier machine. Let it be heavy enough.

I had to let her stand alone for a second, space blanket drawn over her chest and belly, while I covered myself and got my Ski-Doo out of the drift and turned it around.

"I'll sit down facing the front and you sit on top of me facing the back so we can keep our skin together," I said. "I'm going to keep you alive, don't you worry."

Forcibly I brought her with me as I sat and maneuvered her onto my lap. I exposed my chest and stomach again and held her body against mine, her bent knees clutching onto my hips like a jockey on a racing horse. Luckily the seat was big enough to hold two in the awkward position.

My body seemed to welcome her skin after the few moments apart. Could it be that her body was actually warming up, so that my skin could feel an improvement against her body? I held her close and went through fumbled procedures to start the machine.

It was hard to maneuver with one hand, my left one keeping Tess close against me. I took back the gloves and put Tess's exposed hands inside my shirt, along my ribs. The cold seared my sides. It felt as if my guts were wrenching into spasms.

The Ski-Doo rumbled and grumbled and groaned. Finally it took hold and moved, even if slowly. I cheered aloud.

"We're on our way back to the lodge," I shouted. "We're going to make it!"

Please, machine, do your thing, I kept praying. The snowmobile lurched slowly back the way we'd come. But the light snow had started again, obscuring our trail, and I wasn't totally sure of each turn. How much trail had Karl made for us? Was I taking us farther from the lodge instead of closer to safety?

"Shift your body right," I begged Tess when we had to get traction for a turn. She was a dead weight. We took it too wide but somehow made it around the bend, our feet brushing through the banked snow as we barely cleared the turn. The snowmobile's engine whined, scarcely crawling. But we were still moving.

Now I could see the tall angled roof of the lodge ahead through the treetops and I aimed that way in grateful confidence.

"We're going to make it," I kept telling Tess. "Talk to me, tell me you know we're going to make it."

"We're gonna make it," she whispered groggily.

CHAPTER FOURTEEN

The lodge inside felt almost as cold as outside. The furnace wouldn't go on when I twisted the dial of the thermostat on the first floor. No red showed at all on the thermometer. I jostled the dial back and forth, almost wrestling it off the wall. No reassuring whoosh of hot air. Nothing. I tried the kitchen thermostat. Nothing. Bedrooms. Nothing.

"The furnace is out," I said to Tess when I came back downstairs with warm clothes and quilts. I'd half-carried, half-dragged her to the camel corduroy sofa in front of the fireplace while I ran around.

"Must be the storm, huh," I ventured as I helped her into fresh thermal underwear, flannel pajamas, floor-length plush robe, and two pairs of socks. At least the electricity was still on; I raced back upstairs and got her hair dryer and a towel for her head.

"It never went down before," Tess said, teeth still chattering. I found an extension cord in the kitchen and aimed the hair dryer lightly over her face, trying to counteract the gray color on her cheeks. "Ouch, that's too hot," she said, moving her hands to her face.

I'd better find out what I should be doing. The first aid booklet was still outside. I threw one of the quilts over my shoulders and braved the cold.

I checked Tess for all of the hypothermia symptoms as I read. Shivering, yes. Rigid muscles? She'd complained her legs were numb. Excessive fatigue, yes. Lack of coordination, yes. Irrationality, no. Extremities swollen and blue? No, but her legs and arms were kind of gray.

Gray skin was a sign of frostbite. Thaw slowly, or you could get gangrene. That meant amputation. Oh, my God.

The fact that she'd had feeling in her cheeks when I tried the hair dryer was a good sign.

Dilated pupils, yes. I tried to find her pulse and couldn't. Her breaths came half as often as mine.

Signs of impending death: the person becomes unconscious, the pulse slows even more, breathing becomes more labored, and white foam develops at mouth.

"Stay awake," I told Tess. "Talk to me."

The booklet suggested a tepid bath, but I couldn't

get her upstairs. Fuel oil heated our hot water anyway. I could make her tea in the microwave, warm her insides.

I tried to start a fire in the big living room fireplace. Matches jumped out of my hands, lit ones broke and sputtered out, smoke billowed into the room from the crumpled newspapers I'd used, twigs just wouldn't catch.

Once strong flames blanketed the logs, I added a teabag to the microwaved mug of water and brought it to Tess.

"I hate tea, take it away, I bet it's caffeinated," she said. She'd had the same brand with breakfast.

Her chest heaved. I tried to take her pulse again and couldn't find it. Why didn't I have Anne's hands, able to find a pulse on a squirming poodle?

"Tess, I'm going to take your clothes off again and have you lie next to me wrapped up in quilts."

She grumbled that she didn't want me to see her this way, and stumbled on her feet when I tried to get her thermal underwear off. "Leave me alone!" she insisted. "I just want to go to sleep."

"That's exactly what you can't do," I told her.

She resisted, getting angry, saying things that made no sense. "Unhand me, you cow," I think she said at one point.

"Tess, a sign of hypothermia is irrational thinking. You have to let me do this. You have to trust me."

She seemed to pass out. Oh my God, unconscious. Still talking to her, I covered every inch of her skin with my own, my fingers seeking out their counterparts on her hands, my toes attempting to reach all of hers. I tried to breathe my very life into her. I had never been so cold in all my life. My skin burned from the cold.

The thought hit me and I had to laugh grimly to myself: Where were those hot flashes when I needed them?

"I want my tea now," Tess said from deep in the quilt.

Thank God. I got up and brought her the mug, keeping everything but her nostrils covered with the quilts. I kept one quilt for myself and jammed my feet into more socks.

The fire caught hard and sent up a swell of hot flame. Warmth permeated the area in front of the fireplace where we sat. Was it too hot for her? I scooted the sofa a few feet back with her on it, despite her complaints, leaving grooves in the floor finish. We'd worry about that later.

The warmth felt wonderful to me. I was shivering myself. Mentally I ran through the rest of the symptoms against my own condition. Nothing except shivering. I was naked except for the quilt and socks, what did I expect? I put on her long johns. Then her robe.

Her fingers were bright red. Was that a good sign, or was holding the mug too much heat? I took the mug away and gave her the tea in small sips while keeping her hands on my belly under my shirt.

"Hold on to me. Put your feet on top of my legs." I adjusted her on the sofa, tucking her feet inside the legs of my thermal underwear. I absolutely hate someone's cold feet against me.

Now I wondered if I should be using the hair dryer again — people lose a big part of their body heat from the top of their heads, especially if their hair is wet — or whether the heated air would be too much.

I was driving myself crazy, wishing I knew for sure what to do.

"Next time make it Red Zinger," she complained at the next sip of tea.

"I promise, I will." She seemed to pass out again. "Wake up!" I yelled. Her eyes opened wide in terror. I mustn't scare her. "Tess? Do you hear me? It's very important that you talk to me. Tell me where you feel any pain."

She giggled instead. Bad sign.

"Listen, I think the very best thing we can do is for me to lie next to you again." I adjusted her on the sofa again and took off my clothes once more. The quilts kept slipping off of me, dangerously near the flames. My naked skin felt as cold as hers.

Surreptitiously I checked my own fingers and toes — normal pink. I was surviving the exposure. In fact, as the fireplace roared, I was getting too hot. No matter, keeping Tess alive was more important. At least now I had more warmth to give her.

I snuggled close to her like a lover. "See, isn't this nice? Naked dykes together, yum, yum. Red hot lovers."

"What will Hayley say?" she giggled, responding to my joke.

"She'll say, 'Keep that nice woman alive so she can have a music festival and launch my singing comeback.'"

"Okay, I will. She can be my number one performer," Tess mumbled. For a moment I thought she was unconscious again. Then she snored. I listened; her breathing rate seemed normal. And finally I could feel a steady pulse.

I thought sleep was okay, probably good, but I'd have to keep a close watch on her. Best to just stay where I was. My back was hot from the fire and the quilt. My front against her still-cool skin was uncomfortable and itchy. I rolled over and gave her my warm back. Ouch, she was still cold — the sudden contact made me jump away.

Deliberately I forced myself to get close again. I brought her cold hands under my breasts. I wanted nothing more than to pull away and sit by the fire all alone until I was truly warm myself. I stayed with her and promised to reward myself later. I visualized sitting in a warm bath.

Tess still snored lightly. She responded to my questions with reassuring uh huhs and an occasional sane word. Her facial color was near normal. I could almost let myself believe that the worst was over.

When she rolled me off of her and snuggled into her quilt, I dared to leave her for a second to make a call from the kitchen, while I zapped a cup of tea for myself.

As I reached for the phone I almost slapped myself. I should have called first! The ambulance could have been here by now.

I dialed 911. The phone was dead.

All the other phones had no dial tone either.

I couldn't believe it. The storm hadn't seemed *that* bad. No electrical storms, no raging winds to tear down lines, just falling snow. The fuel oil furnace and the phones both? But Tess had complained about the phone lines going down in a bad thunderstorm during the summer. Maybe it was just the weight of the snow pulling down a line.

Of course the fax and e-mail were dead since they depended on the phone lines.

My car phone! I wrapped the quilt around me again on top of the robe and shoved my double-socked feet into another pair of boots. I was changing clothes more often than a model on a catwalk.

In preparation for the snowstorm, we'd put the cars in the garage alongside the snowmobiles. As I raced toward both our cars, something seemed strange. They seemed to sit funny. What was wrong? Immediately I saw the answer. All eight tires were flat.

Before I looked inside the Jeep, I already knew the phone was destroyed. No question now, this was no act of nature.

Snowmobile trail aimed over the lake, furnace out, no phones. Was somebody out to kill Tess? Or me? Or both of us?

And they probably weren't through.

CHAPTER FIFTEEN

I was going to have to go for help. On the snowmobile. With Tess. I couldn't leave her behind, while the attempted murderer was who knows where, doing who knows what? Maybe lurking in the lodge. Maybe waiting on the road.

I went back to Tess. She seemed to be sleeping nicely. Now I could find her pulse easily and it was eighty beats a minute. But I still didn't like the color of her feet, hands and nose. I didn't know what I should do — stay here by the fire and risk Tess getting gangrene from untreated frostbite, or leave for help, risking further damage from the cold?

I reread the first aid booklet. Shock should be my next concern, it said. She had none of the signs. I sat with her for a while, torn between the need to stay and the need to leave.

"Tess, the phone lines are down," I said to her when she shifted positions. "Tess, do you hear me?"

For a second she opened her eyes and smiled. "I'm going to be okay, aren't I?"

"Yes, you are, but I want to have a doctor check you over. You don't want to lose any toes or fingers."

She shuddered again, then smiled. "Not gonna happen. I'm going to be okay. Eh?" The last syllable was added deliberately, an attempt to get me to smile back.

"Yah," I said, in a Yooper drawl that made her laugh aloud. Good. "You're going to be okay. But the phone lines are down, and we're going to have to go for help. Someone vandalized the cars too. We're going to have to leave on my snowmobile. Do you think you can make it?"

Her eyes opened wide and she shuddered. "The cars too? Somebody . . ."

"I think so. We're in danger here. We could be in danger on the road too. But you could get gangrene and die if we stay here. We're going to have to bundle up."

As I dressed us again in all those layers, I kept going over who could be responsible for this catastrophe.

The obvious pick was Karl Thorsdal, Rita's brother, who had groomed the snowmobile trails. Tess may have thought he was an okay guy, but what if he was furious at what she had done to his sister, blaming Tess for Rita's change in lifestyle? Maybe he felt his sister had abandoned her family, had abandoned him?

But he was too obvious a choice. He'd have to know he'd be the first suspect. Someone had to have made it look like his work.

Or was he pulling a *Basic Instinct,* a Sharon Stone saying that she wasn't that dumb to do something that she'd obviously be blamed for, to cover up the fact that she'd really done it. Or was he so dumb — or enraged — that he hadn't even thought about anyone arresting him? Maybe he'd assumed we'd both go into the lake and drown and never be found until spring, if then? There was probably no law against making a snowmobile trail over a lake that was at least partially frozen already. I imagined a snow groomer had to be heavier than a snowmobile, so somebody had had to use something lighter, like a snow blower, or else use salt on the ice afterward to weaken it more.

Half the people in town had heard Tess tell Thal Swanson we'd be going snowmobiling in the morning when we'd all picked up last-minute provisions at the convenience store. And Thal made no attempt to hide his loathing.

I couldn't help scanning the horizon. Not to mention imagining the bullet that could come from behind any tree. I wondered if the bullets that had narrowly missed us a few weeks ago had actually been from deer hunters, or from this same madman?

Or madwoman? Don't rule out women automatically, I told myself. But which one? Ardith

Underwood, in her Wal-Mart greeter's costume? She wouldn't let her hair get mussed. I had too many men who were better candidates to consider. Like maybe her husband. He might be sixty, but if he had the right equipment, he'd be capable of faking a snowmobile path over the lake.

I had the passing insight that in the country, you see people of all ages doing what they have to, staying active, whereas in L.A. the ages are so segregated that you rarely see what elderly people can accomplish. After meeting Rudy, I'd never underestimate older people again. Maybe even myself.

The engine revved and took off. But where to? I wasn't sure I knew the way to Ironwood alone, and it was too far anyway, though it had the resources I needed. Where was the nearest working phone? Camp Tessel was my best bet. At the moment I didn't even rule out Hank Gerlock as the attempted murderer, no matter how nice he'd been to Tess. I drove in large circles in the parking lot, getting my bearings, while I thought. Camp Tessel still had the closest phone. I took off, Tess hanging on behind me.

Hadn't Tess said that the lawyers had fought for years over where the Foundation ended and her share of the fortune began? She thought everyone had reached a peaceful resolution, but maybe not. I wanted a look at the will myself, maybe have Kitt's resources examine it for loopholes. As if the best lawyers in the country hadn't already done that.

And what about that uncle and aunt Tess had, her father's brother and sister, who got less from their grandfather's will than she did? The woman was a nun — rule her out. No, not so quickly, not without checking. What had Tess said about the uncle? He needed money to buy the company stock? They'd have had the best lawyers on their side too.

It seemed much farther down the road than when we'd driven the distance in my Jeep. I kept track of the chain link fence as a guide as I sped over the road, wishing that the snowplows would make a repeat appearance and take me to a phone.

Finally I saw the camouflage-painted Camp Tessel sign and turned down the gravel road and into the parking lot. No sign of the white Land Rover — I hoped it was in the garage and Gerlock was home — but there was a smaller car, a maroon Cavalier with a yellow rental tag in the window. Somebody had to be there.

The snowplows had plowed Camp Tessel even longer ago than the hunting lodge, and I pumped the throttle with my thumb to keep up speed so I wouldn't sink in the deep soft snow. So when I tried to stop at the low red brick building I almost crashed into the wall. The Ski-Doo sank into a drift at a twenty-degree angle, nose down. It was going to be really hard to dig it out from there.

"Tess? Can you get up?" I cried.

"I'm stuck," she said. "My leg's caught under something."

Someone had better be home. I leaned on the snowmobile's horn, a vacuous toot. I floundered around in the snow before I discovered the metal door Tess had gone through on our previous visit, and I pounded on it with my fists. No response. No doorbell was visible. Snow buried the camera lens. I wiped it clean and pounded again.

I thought I saw a faint light glowing around the edges of one mini-blind-covered window, and smoke curled out of a metal chimney pipe emerging from the roof. In the emergency kit I found a small wrench and hit the door repeatedly with it, metal striking metal.

"What's going on here?" The flat, German-accented voice boomed out of a speaker above the door.

"I'm Laney Samms from the Tessel Lodge down the road, and Tess Cutler is in serious trouble," I yelled into the speaker. "She fell into the lake on her snowmobile and she may have frostbite. Our phone lines are down and I need to call for help. I've got her here — she needs to get inside where it's warm."

The steel door lumbered ajar. A tall gray-haired man with ruddy cheeks, struggling to force a parka over a floor-length green velour robe, bare legs jammed into boots, followed me to the snowmobile. He lifted a corner of the machine off of Tess while I pulled her out.

"How's your leg?" I asked her.

"It's okay, not broken. Bruised some." She half-walked, half-leaned her way inside on Gerlock's arm.

We were in an eight-foot square room that my Michigan relatives had called a mud room, a place to kick the snow off of boots and leave a dripping umbrella and hang up your coat, and also to keep the cold wind from sweeping through the entire house when the outside door was opened. The right wall was coat hangers and wood-slatted benches. To the left was an all-glass door that opened to a room apparently designed to register guests to the camp; a wood counter with a few piles of papers ran the entire length of the room.

Ahead of us a wood door opened to what seemed

like the parlor of a country inn — golden hardwood floors and walls, a round braided rug, chintz-covered overstuffed sofas, a rocking chair and fireplace. Not exactly what I'd expected. Gerlock sat Tess down on the sofa and wrapped her in an afghan and examined her closely. He had the look of a physician in the way he checked her eyes and pulse.

I reached for the phone. One button of the four lines was lit and I punched another to dial 911. "An ambulance will take too long," he said, hanging up the phone on me. "I'll drive us to the hospital. By the way, I'm Hank Gerlock."

"Laney Samms," I said again. We shook hands.

"Darling? Is something wrong?"

A cool blonde swimming in a robe that matched his appeared in another door at the rear of the parlor. She was brushing her shoulder-length straight hair. This guy was no hermit.

"I'm going to have to go out for a bit," he said.

"But you promised you wouldn't leave me all weekend!" the woman said, letting her hairbrush draw a golden tress across her face, the strands releasing from the brush one shimmering lock at a time. The effect was like a fan held seductively over her lower face, only her eyes conveying their tempting message. Her eyes were maple syrup brown.

"I know, but there's been a terrible accident and I have to take someone to the hospital." He reached down and kissed her. He had to work to unwrap himself from her arms. "Some things can't be helped. Oh, Miss . . . Samms? This is Angelique Silva, who is visiting this country from her native Brazil." Now I could see he was quite a good-looking man, in a Cary

Grant kind of way. No wonder this gorgeous young woman was here.

She sighed and wrapped the large robe around her size four body. "It's an extended visit. I'm a graduate student at the University of Chicago. I met Hank at a seminar in telecommunications last week and had to see his set-up for myself." She extended a hand. Her shake was firm and friendly, accompanied by wafts of some expensive perfume. Her smile came off of a *Vogue* cover.

"You'll excuse me for a moment while I get dressed." Hank disappeared into the same room from which Angelique had come and closed the door. Hank gone, Angelique stood there, arms at her sides, not even bothering to pout anymore, looking back longingly at the bedroom. Not even going to Tess's side in the most basic human gesture of comforting someone in trouble.

I checked on Tess myself, and she seemed much improved. The worst seemed to be over. I relaxed a bit and looked around my surroundings. To the left was another room, door ajar, from which emanated a glow. Attempting to be discreet, I moved over a few steps to see inside.

He had a fifteen-inch color monitor. I edged closer and tried to read the text. The screen went blank — Windows' built-in screen saver. He apparently didn't bother with flying toasters. I was dying to press a key and see what he'd been working on, but I don't read other people's mail either. Besides, with my luck, I'd probably accidentally erase a week's work. And Angelique was now watching me.

It seems acceptable to look at people's

bookshelves. On a shelf above the computer were mainly software manuals, interspersed with boxes of CDs and floppies. I smiled at the first title on another shelf of VHS tapes: *Winning Paintball*. The next was interesting: *The Navy Seal Workout Challenge*. But my smile faded at some of the other titles. *Green Berets — The Fighting Men. Great Combat Handguns. Ambush! Navy Seals in Deadly Action. Inside S.W.A.T.* Maybe he'd been in the Seals, Green Berets or a police S.W.A.T. unit. Or maybe he used these resources for his survivalist training classes. I let out a shallow breath.

Across the room were shelves of books. One large title was readable to me: *Rommel — The Desert Fox*. Another smaller-print title was decorated with a swastika. I shuddered and tried to catch other titles but got only the impression that this guy was infatuated with World War II. I'd forced myself to pay attention to some of the documentaries of that period which have been appearing regularly in the news since the fifty-year anniversary of Pearl Harbor, but it was hard to do. Not for this guy, apparently. I'd been born during that war. Gerlock must have been just a kid. Maybe his father had filled his head with war stories and started his interest. I'd met some otherwise decent men who seemed infatuated with military history. Look at the success of the Rambo-type films. I couldn't help thinking of the recent best-seller, *Men Are From Mars, Women Are From Venus*.

A bank of fourteen-inch monitors filled another shelf. Maybe they were part of a security system surveying the camp, but they were all turned off. Guess he hadn't been watching the screens when I was pounding at the door. Or maybe he used them to watch the proceedings of the paintball games.

Another wall was a blue screen, the kind movie makers use for special effects, and a video camera and fancy lighting completed the stage. An expensive suit jacket, shirt and tie hung on a wood hanger alongside the blue screen. I envisioned Gerlock taping himself in the suit in front of the blue screen and projecting an image of Camp Tessel behind him. Given the stack of VCRs, I figured he taped his own promotional videos for the business. He controlled the whole Tessel Foundation from this room; I wonder how many people knew that? So why bother with this paintball hobby? Why not relax with golf or fishing? I noticed a stack of his business cards in a holder on his desk and pocketed one.

He reappeared in a Shetland sweater, corduroy slacks and boots, and stepped into the one-piece copper-colored jumpsuit he'd brought with him. He followed my gaze into his computer room and looked annoyed. "Excuse me again," he said, and went over to the computer and turned it off. I noticed a second line lit up on the Merlin business phone on the table in front of me in the parlor. He closed the office door firmly behind him.

Angelique was pouting again.

"Don't whine, darling, it isn't becoming," he said, planting a kiss a few inches away from her face. "I'll be back very soon. It can't be helped. I know I promised I'd be with you all weekend."

So he'd been busy overnight. Unless this little scene had been staged. At this point I didn't feel I had much choice but to trust him. The two of us maneuvered Tess to the Land Rover and got her into the back seat; I joined her there to put her hands back inside my clothing to counteract the latest blast of cold she'd received. The car took off like a dream through the snow. I couldn't believe the speedometer read seventy when I glanced over at the dash just seconds later.

"You say the phone lines are down, and the furnace?"

I gave him a fuller story of what had happened.

He had his own car phone with a built-in directory. He called up several numbers. First he punched in the number for Grand View Hospital and ordered them to have Doctor O'Hanrahan present when he arrived with a hypothermia patient in about fifteen minutes.

Next he called an Ironwood garage and ordered eight new tires to be brought to Tessel Lodge and installed on our two cars. He had to ask me for their makes and years. "They know me — I'll guarantee the bill and have it put on my account and we'll settle later," he said to Tess, who nodded. "Of course we'll pay extra for overtime," he said into the phone, looking to Tess for confirmation. "The roads are clear, you can make it fine."

The same no-nonsense tone ordered the phone company to fix our lines immediately, even if it was the weekend, and a furnace company to get heat going again at the lodge, no matter what it took.

"No, it can't wait until morning."

Finally he called the State Police in Wakefield and insisted upon talking to Detective Cyprian Lamppa. He spoke quietly, telling the officer all that I had told him. "Be sure and check out the spot where the

164

snowmobile went into the lake," he said. "Treat it as a crime scene."

After our experiences with the Beer Barrel and Ironwood officers, I was surprised at the way the policeman on the other end seemed to be taking him seriously. State police generally did get better training, I supposed. I wondered if the Beer Barrel part-timer had had any training at all.

By then we were at Grand View.

CHAPTER SIXTEEN

Tess was going to be fine, doctors told me later that evening. The specialist Gerlock had ordered to be on hand reassured me that she wouldn't lose any fingers or toes, and that she could go home in the morning. Monday morning. Kitt was arriving at Ironwood Wednesday afternoon.

Dr. O'Hanrahan even gave me the once-over and pronounced me in good condition, not to worry over the aches and pains I'd probably feel in the morning. I said I'd wait for Tess to be released.

Gerlock left after talking to the doctor. "I'll have

your car here for you in the morning," Hank said. I couldn't even force myself to politely decline, to say that he'd done too much already, that we'd get home somehow. I was too tired to even thank him properly. I slept on the cracked leatherette benches with chrome pipe armrests that passed as waiting room seating.

As promised, there was my Jeep in the parking lot when Tess was discharged. And I was sore all over. My skin felt as if I'd fallen asleep in a tanning booth. I bought Advil at the hospital pharmacy and took three tablets.

Gerlock had paid the bill in advance, leaving a note that Tess could settle with him later if she insisted — he didn't think she'd had an insurance card or wallet with her when she'd checked in. He would prefer that she accept his help without even thinking about paying him back.

Why was he doing all this?

"Just being nice, I guess." Tess was willing to give him the benefit of the doubt. The only signs of her ordeal were a few bandages on her hands and bruises on her arms. "Hey, when you have money, it's no big thing to spend a little here and there."

"Right, like in hundred-thousand-dollar checks for parking lots."

"Exactly," she said, looking smug, my point passing her by completely.

I wasn't sure just what my point was — that she and Gerlock shouldn't be spending their money, letting the banks continue to have full use of it while ignoring the possibilities of doing good with it? Maybe she was right. I just didn't understand how people could spend big chunks of money without agonizing over the decision, without having to take into consideration what's in it for them. Class differences, I guessed. Tess had never hurt for money growing up, never had to balance shut-off notice deadlines. Gerlock either, I was sure. What was in it for him to be so nice to us anyway?

"Don't worry about it, just accept it," Tess said. She was feeling joyous, if groggy. "Thank you, thank you, thank you!" she said to me, over and over again. "I'm going to give you that trip to Tahiti when this is all over."

She breathed deeply, enjoying the crisp morning. "It's great to be alive! Promise, I'll never force you to go snowmobiling again. I don't think I will, either. I still don't understand how I could have gone through the ice that way."

It was time to tell her my suspicions about her "accident."

When we drove into the lodge parking lot there was a navy and gold Michigan State Police car at our door.

I looked over Detective Cyprian Lamppa and guessed that he took after his Greek ancestors on his mother's side who'd given him his first name rather than his paternal Finn side. Stocky build, maybe five-ten, maybe thirty-five. Coarse black wavy hair, thick black moustache. Steady, intelligent, deep-set brown eyes, olive complexion. Posture like a Canadian Mountie.

I cracked a joke and his glance withered my laugh to nothingness. No lip given or allowed. He went over every detail of what had happened with us, including listing every person we could remember who had been at the convenience store Saturday night.

I also told him about the shootings during deer season and decided to mention the car bomb incident back in L.A. "I think somebody is trying to kill Tess," I concluded.

He made a phone call to get more information, sitting himself down in the kitchen with a pad and pencil and a fresh cup of coffee he'd brewed himself in our Mr. Coffee.

Yes, the phones worked again. So did the furnace. I started a new fire to supplement the heat to the living room. Outside, it was even colder today, barely above zero degrees Farenheit, with a wind chill factor dropping it to minus twelve. There was much to be grateful for.

"Your mad bomber was caught in New York a few days ago," he announced when he hung up about a half hour later. "He attempted to wire the car of an Israeli diplomat, but purely by luck the FBI was already watching the area for another reason and nabbed him in the act. So this job couldn't have been him. Besides, a car bomber would have wired the snowmobiles, not made a trail over a lake."

That made sense to me. Somehow I'd hoped this case was tied to the other, not a whole new set of bad guys to worry about. I'd have to call Kitt to see if she'd heard the news.

Lamppa wanted the whole story. I told him that Tess and I were lesbians, that we were putting together a women's music festival for the lodge, that we would be bringing hundreds, maybe thousands, of lesbians onto the property in the summer, and that she'd met with some resistance from local residents. He didn't flinch or squirm a bit; I was watching.

Tess showed him a copy of the letter to the *Globe* from Reverend Mark Hudspeth saying we'd be bringing in gay men for orgies. With minor embarrassment she recounted her romance with Rita Swanson, ex-wife of Thal, sister of Karl. I added the story about Joe Underwood's saying we were going to destroy the town's future, such as it was. The trooper simply wrote it all down, uttering a few "hmms" along the way.

As we recounted the incidents, none of them seemed serious enough to be a forerunner of anything more than vandalism, harassment, prejudice and fear-mongering. And if that were enough to instigate murder, there'd be no one in L.A. left alive. Maybe nobody left on earth.

"We've got quite a bit to check out," Detective Lamppa said. "We took samples this morning from the area where your snowmobile went into the water. Someone definitely detoured the trail. Even though the snow kept falling, you can tell where the trail was blocked and a new one made in the direction of the lake. The real trail continues on the other side of the snowbank roadblock, but you couldn't see it when you were low in your snowmobiles."

I looked at Tess. Finally she seemed to realize our situation.

"How could somebody make a trail without a snow groomer?" she asked. "Isn't Karl the only one with a snow groomer around, except maybe the ones at the ski lodges at Porcupine Mountain and Big Powderhorn?"

"There are a few others. Even the little ski lodges

have them. And the snowmobile clubs. But I think the damage was done with one of the snowplows or snow blowers in your garage."

"I'd wondered if that was possible," I said.

"It would take a lot longer, but yes, someone with a small machine could do the same job as a big snowplow and a groomer. He'd know it was snowing enough to cover his handiwork. We found a few drops of oil in the banked snow on the phony trail. We're sending the sample to a lab in Lansing, along with samples of oil from the equipment in your garage that looked as if it might have been used lately."

"Isn't it all the same oil?" I asked. "When Karl went over the machines in the garage, wouldn't he have used the same oil on them all?"

"Maybe, maybe not. But even if he did, each motor adds its own little contaminants. It's practically like DNA testing, only you don't have to grow the genes. We're going to talk to these folks" — he looked down at his notebook — "and see what they have to say." He made a few more notes. "You have to know that this may be simple vandalism or malicious mischief," he said finally. "The cumulative effects of the damage to your cars and utilities and the new snowmobile trail led to a serious situation, and yes, Tess could have died. But if we do catch the culprit, we might not be able to pin anything serious on him. You have to understand that. You really shouldn't be throwing around words like murder."

He was getting that superior tone that drives me nuts. "If someone cuts your brake linings and you die as a result, isn't that murder?" I said.

He gave us a cool look. "Each case is up to the

courts to decide. All I can tell you is that we don't have much crime around here, and so we're going all out on your case. Meanwhile, you two sit tight and get well. I think we've deflected the *Globe*—no reporters should bother you."

Tess and I looked at each other — I hadn't thought of that aspect yet. Gerlock had, the detective told us. And I was supposed to be the PR specialist. I made a note to call Wanda at the *Globe* myself to touch base.

"We wrote up the police report like a minor snowmobile accident," Lamppa continued. "No sense getting the whole county up in arms. You might read a few paragraphs about your 'accident' in the paper — anything you do is big news, Tess, even falling in a lake. Don't trip in the bathtub."

"Why is Hank Gerlock doing all this for us?" I had to ask, while Tess nudged at me as if I were making a social blunder. This was an investigation — no niceties necessary.

"He's a genuinely nice guy." Lamppa shrugged. "He uses his money well. Not something that could always be said for old man Tessel."

"So why does he bother with this paramilitary thing?" Lamppa didn't seem to understand what I meant. "I mean the paintball thing. Why is he mixed up with a bunch of revolutionary wannabes?" Tess looked really embarrassed on my behalf.

"All I can tell you is that Hank has many sides, and one of them is enjoyment of the outdoors. He hit upon a new craze in paintball, and he does it for fun," Lamppa said as he wrote. "Paintball isn't for survivalists anymore. Families do it, civic groups do it. It's a great fundraiser for churches and community organizations. He hires a lot of local people to actually run the events, but you'll find him in goggles and cammies — camouflage clothes — playing with the best of them. It's absolutely harmless fun — you ought to try it sometime."

"Have you?"

The detective smiled, his heavy black moustache twitching in amusement. "Yes. I did. With my sons, at a benefit for the Policemen's Benevolent Association. I even got my wife into cammies and she shot a few rounds. Not too bad a shot, either, she found out. So you're way out of line if you think Hank Gerlock is behind any of this. You have my word on that."

Somewhere I filed away my suspicions. I still didn't trust Gerlock, despite the glowing testimonial, and despite Lamppa's apparent professionalism. Do cynics live longer? Or die younger from stress?

Lamppa's moustache twitched again. "If you think of anything else give me a call." He handed me his card.

"You say your friend is coming in from Los Angeles Wednesday? Having another person around is good. I'll assign a car to drive by several times a day to keep an eye out on you. This guy might come back."

"You don't think it was Karl, do you?" Tess asked. "He's always been so nice to me. He keeps saying how much happier Rita is now."

"It's hard to say at this point. I wouldn't rule anyone out."

"Uh, could I ask you one more question?" Lamppa turned to me. "Was Gerlock ever in the Navy Seals or the Green Berets?"

173

The trooper gave me a tight smile. "I'm unaware of his previous background. You might want to ask him yourself." He left.

"What was that all about?" Tess asked. I told her about Gerlock's library. She merely said, "Men, they all love that kind of junk. Like Schwartzenegger films."

When I called Wanda, I didn't say anything more than what Gerlock had told the papers, but I did ask her if she had any information on Gerlock himself. "He's been so . . . nice, overly nice, since the accident that I keep wondering about him. Since he's right next door to the lodge, it makes me a little nervous."

"He's never been in any kind of trouble that I heard," the reporter said. "Is something else going on that I should know about?"

I debated. "No, just that I have a tingling feeling that makes me a little worried. You know the feeling?"

"Sure do. Usually there's a reason for it, too. I'll keep my ears open, okay?"

"Thanks." I hung up.

Tess and I tried to think over the past few weeks in more detail. For the life of us, we couldn't come up with a thing additional to tell the police. Sighting the occasional scout car making the rounds on our roads would be unsettling and only a little reassuring.

We talked about hiring a security guard and couldn't find any listed in the phone book, and a few calls didn't turn up any such service in Gogebic County. A different world from L.A. We debated calling around in Duluth and Minneapolis and decided that the scout car patrols would be good enough.

We'd be a little more alert, that's all. A lot more alert.

When I put my hand in my pocket later I came across Gerlock's business card. He had a phone number and an e-mail address. Across the bottom was another number, handwritten. I dialed it and heard the familiar sound of, presumably, a fax modem. Of course. There was no fax number printed on the card. But just out of curiosity, I fooled around on my notebook. The number led into a bulletin board service.

All the current postings were shocking — people ranting with every dirty word they could think of, attacking Jews, Israel and "sympathizers." I'd never seen such shit. I couldn't take any more and got out as fast as I could. There aren't many bulletin boards for gays. Some feminists I know have found great chat lines that they enjoy a lot, but I keep running into the stupid ones, even the ones which are supposedly by and for lesbians. I've heard more intelligent conversation from parakeets.

Tess and I rolled around in that big lodge the rest of the day and the next like the last peas left in a soup bowl, waiting the reappearance of the spoon.

Tess felt totally well by Wednesday, ready to drive with me to Ironwood to pick up Kitt. "Besides, I don't want to be left alone," she explained. I could understand that. We waved at the state trooper who was coming up our driveway as we drove out. He waved back and kept going.

Gogebic County Airport consists of three small white sheds passing as hangars, a gray stone and aluminum siding control center, and a one-story red brick terminal. United Express has six arrivals and departures a day, and each plane seats nineteen to thirty-one passengers. You park twenty feet from the terminal's front door. No long-term parking lots, no shuttle buses, no at-the-curb luggage check-ins, no crowds. I could almost enjoy flying if all airports were this size.

Kitt came in from Chicago, wearing a camelhair chesterfield coat that was no match for the current twelve-degree U.P. weather. Gusty winds almost blew the coat off of her as she came down the metal airplane stairs. Her hair stood straight out as if she'd been shot through with lightning.

"Holy shit, it's cold!" she yelled over the wind when we spotted her.

"We'd already noticed," I yelled back.

We got her to the Cherokee ASAP. Always-prepared Tess had brought a thick parka, face mask, fur-lined gloves and flannel-lined jeans from my wardrobe for Kitt to put on as we drove. Kitt waved away all but the parka and gloves. Her hair still bushed around her — her hairdresser never gave her all that body. She had enough big hair to be a televangelist.

"So what's the big hurry for me to get here?" she asked. I could sense that she was trying not to look down her nose too obviously at the hick towns we passed. Her lips moved and the corners of her mouth twitched at the signs: "Ernest Erne, Hitch Repair." "Lila's Home-Made Pasties." The "lisensed plummer."

The nuclear family deer statues and gaudy steel butterflies now capped in snow.

"*Quaint* is the word you're looking for," I said. She flushed, caught again in her snobbery.

"There's a new fly in the ointment, Kitt. Something more has happened." Kitt jerked her head. I turned to Tess. "Do you want to tell her, or should I?"

"Oh, you go ahead. I was out of it most of the time."

I gave Kitt the whole story. She put her hands over her ears at one point, refusing to believe it. "You're a weathervane for trouble," she said to me at one point.

"Oh sure, blame the victim," I retorted. "Who got me into this mess in the first place?"

Kitt also didn't believe the size and luxury of the lodge when we pulled up. Nor that Officer Lamppa was waiting for us. The introductions were cursory.

"And how long are you planning on staying?" Lamppa did ask Kitt.

"Just a few days," she said.

"And what are your plans now?" He turned to Tess and me.

"Not much longer for me," I said.

"When exactly?"

"Oh . . ." I looked at Tess. "The fifteenth?"

"Probably," she said. "Maybe longer for me. I keep having this urge to spend the winter here, just to say I did it. Plus I kind of like the idea of doing some winter music projects here next year, maybe have an ongoing college credit course. Maybe it could be broadcast on public television . . ."

I rolled my eyes. "See, Kitt? She keeps coming up with one idea after another, and I'm trying to get her to commit to a simple plan first, just to get started."

Kitt tilted her head at Tess. "We'll work it out, won't we?" Tess smiled back.

Lamppa looked a little sick. He took a step forward that caused both of them to retreat a few inches. "To get back to my job . . ."

He looked in each of our faces. I recognized the subtle ploy to regain the power of being the focus of attention. Body English is fascinating to me. I'd take a step forward myself, do a little posturing, but it wasn't worth it. Sometimes I like to experiment with confronting a male ego in ways that the guy doesn't even know why he's uncomfortable, his unconscious body language isn't getting its expected response. But Lamppa was just doing his job, and I didn't want to interfere even slightly.

"The oil sample checked out with one of your snowblowers," he said. "And most of our suspects were all together in one room having a late-night poker game till all hours. Not Karl, of course, but he did a whole lot of plowing that night all over the county. He had to have stayed on schedule to get it done. He did make a special pass from the Underwoods' house to let the poker players go home on clear roads."

"How convenient, they're each other's alibis?" I said.

"You got it."

"Maybe it's like *The Orient Express* and they all

did it together," Kitt wisecracked. Lamppa looked at her. Instant mutual dislike, I could see. And she hadn't even stood in his face.

"Could be. But we have no indication that this is murder, ma'am. Probably just malicious mischief. There's been no murder here."

Kitt, a ma'am. She narrowed her eyes. He ignored her.

"We're going to keep on checking," Lamppa said to me. Turning to Tess, he said, "I have to look around inside some more, do you mind?"

Tess and I gave him the tour at the same time we showed Kitt around. Explaining that the first fingerprinting attempts had been futile, Lamppa tried to take additional fingerprints off of the garage door, the snowblowers, and the fuel oil tanks, which had been clogged with dirt.

When he went out to the phone lines, he said he had no hopes of finding any prints except phone company employees, but he'd try anyway. "The phone company says the lines were working again when the repairmen got here. The lines weren't cut, as we suspected. They have no explanation as to what happened."

The officer who had conducted the first tests wasn't as experienced as he should have been, Lamppa apologized — "We don't have much call for fingerprinting around here. That's why I'm repeating the tests myself."

With the continuing light snow, this effort was useless as well.

"The only clear prints we have are of Karl, who

had a legitimate reason to be in the garage. Outside, no prints survived, though anyone would've worn gloves in this weather," he surmised.

We walked around to the rear truck loading ramp which led down to the fuel tanks.

"Someone poured regular garden dirt into the tanks through a funnel." Lamppa pointed to the lids to the fill holes which had been crimped by a clumsily turned wrench. "Hank Gerlock got somebody to spend most of the night pumping the fuel out, filtering it, and flushing out the tanks a few times. That must have cost a pretty penny."

I looked at Tess. "He's been paying for everything. Doesn't this make him the prime suspect?"

"Why, because he's been good to a neighbor?" the trooper interjected.

Lamppa kept on defending Gerlock, who might still be a suspect if that Angelique was lying, even though he'd been so nice to us. At this point I didn't trust anyone.

"He can afford it, everybody knows that," Lamppa continued. "He's just being friendly. He's probably trying to find out what happened on his own, using his own resources we know nothing about. He knows just about everyone you ever heard of through that computer thing he does."

"I'm not sure I'd want friends like that," Kitt interrupted. "Sounds weird to me." Kitt, the one who runs her own kingdom. Rather, queendom. And who has never hesitated to use her own methods and bring in additional help even if it means some people feel she's calling them inadequate. She usually is.

"He's a genuinely nice guy, once you get to know him," Lamppa insisted.

Kitt obviously shared the skepticism I tried to keep hidden. "I don't care, keep checking him out too," Kitt said. Tess and I didn't contradict her.

Lamppa gave Kitt a look that said he was in charge here, don't go giving him any orders. Kitt's stance said that she was always in charge, no matter where she was, no matter who he was.

Quickly I escorted Lamppa to his car while Tess took Kitt to her upstairs suite. I thanked the detective again for all that he had done. In response, he gave a sideways glance toward the second-story window where the lights had just gone on. "What's her role in all this, anyway?"

"She's my boss, Kitt Meyers, owner of a major music distribution company that specializes in women's music and that also puts on special events for the women's community and handles some talent. Tess hired her, and me, to help her put together this women's music festival I mentioned."

"She's not in Los Angeles anymore," he said as he slammed the door to his squad car.

CHAPTER SEVENTEEN

I joined Kitt and Tess upstairs. To my surprise, Tess had invited Kitt to share her suite, and Kitt had accepted. Okay, okay, of course grown women can share a king-sized bed and nothing sexual has to happen, and I could understand why Tess would prefer to have someone in her room with her after the snowmobile incident.

But I wondered why she hadn't asked me to spend the night in her room, Monday and Tuesday nights as well as tonight? I was the logical one, I was the one who had stripped naked and clung to her in a mound of quilts while she drew on my warmth and strength. Not that I had any desire to sleep with Tess, of course.

A light dawned. How dense could I be! I started to watch for any little interplays between the two of them. Subtle, but the glances, the accidental touches, the flushed cheeks, were all there. And as I remembered our last phone conversation, Kitt had said she was ready for something new. Someone new, apparently.

Why was I so surprised? I analyzed my feelings and came to the shameful realization that, to me, Tess's weight had put her out of the running as a potential sex partner and lover. Admittedly, my body had gone onto automatic and I'd felt a touch of tingling during our romp in the quilts, when my main concern was keeping her alive. A few hours rubbing naked bodies together in front of a fireplace can't help but arouse a few nerve endings here and there, despite the overwhelming fears and tension.

But more importantly, as I looked back on the few weeks I'd spent with Tess, I had to see that she was a very desirable woman. I'd follow her blueberry pancakes anywhere, and she had a great sense of humor, not to mention a therapist's trained insights. She had more energy than most thin people, hitting the snowmobile trails and hiking through the woods. She had deep convictions and a desire to help the community in whatever way she could. And she wasn't just going to rest on her money, she was working hard to do something fabulous for underserved Midwest lesbians and performers.

Her perky red haircut was adorable, her eyes were gorgeous, and she had her own sense of style, crazy as her floral jumpers looked to me. No wonder Kitt was going to spend the night with Tess. If I'd had any sense, I'd have realized that Tess was a far better choice for a relationship than my ditzy Hayley Malone. Shut my mouth and slap my face, I said to myself quickly.

"Look what I brought from L.A.," Kitt announced as she unpacked, unwrapping a ceramic menorah. "My parents bought it in Israel from a student at Bezalel." She looked as if I should recognize the name. "Bezalel, the Jerusalem art institute. Bezalel was the artist in the Torah who painted the Ark of the Covenant which the Jews carried with them in the desert," she explained for my benefit. "Tonight's the first night of Hanukkah. I don't celebrate many holidays, but somehow this one seems symbolic."

The menorah was of sea blues and greens flowing fluidly together along the candle holders, the watercolor-like glazes giving a hint of female forms, of mermaids maybe, of women frolicking in the sea.

"It's lovely," Tess said. "My family's menorah is of antique silver carved with scenes from the Torah. My mother promised it to me when she's gone."

"Our family has one like that too, but I wanted a different kind of feeling. For some reason this year, I felt like celebrating. Especially in view of what's happened here. Do you mind lighting the first candle tonight?"

Kitt was talking to Tess. Was I being excluded from a Jewish tradition I didn't share, or were the two of them merely caught in those first stages of a relationship where no one exists in the world except the two of them?

"It would be wonderful," Tess said. "Laney, you

know about Hanukkah." Her words were to me — at least I was being included, but her eyes stayed on Kitt. Uh huh.

"All I know is that you light a new candle each night until you have eight of them, and you're supposed to give gifts on the first night."

"No gifts — that's a tradition that sprung up when Jews felt pressured by their kids to have a holiday similar to Christmas so that the kids could have presents too," Tess said. "Hanukkah just happens to usually fall in December."

"So do we have this ceremony after dinner?"

"Right, after sunset. I'm going to whip up some latkes — potato pancakes — for dinner and then we'll light the candles at dusk, okay?" Tess was speaking to Kitt. Only sporadically did I exist. The two of them went downstairs to the kitchen.

I sat down on my bed and contemplated this new state of affairs. More power to them — Kitt hadn't been involved with anybody in a long time. Her work always comes first. And at least she could be sure Tess wasn't after her money. I wouldn't even let myself think that the opposite might be true. Kitt does have some integrity.

So why was I pissed? Immaturity at being left out? Probably. The third person always feels superfluous. I'd adjust — it was sudden, that's all. You can't help feeling close to someone whose life you've saved, but Tess's attention was totally on Kitt. So she already thanked me, nitwit, I told myself. What do you expect her to do, grovel in gratitude for the rest of her life?

My Higher Power was hovering somewhere around the fringes of this conversation with myself, waiting

185

to get in a sensible word. I kept Her out of it, preferring to wallow in my self-pity. At least for a few minutes more.

The phone rang. I answered it first. My annoyance came out in my voice. "Yeah, what do you want?" I snarled, for no real reason.

"Laney?" The rich, warm voice was tentative but unmistakable.

"Hayley!" I shrieked. Contain yourself, woman, I said silently. "Hayley, how good to hear from you," I added in well-modulated tones.

"I had to go to L.A. to check on the filming of the TV movie on my life, but they've had so many problems they scrapped it."

"What!"

"Part of the problem was the *Vanity Fair* article, which pretty much outed me."

"Uh oh. I didn't see it." Not a trendy magazine rack or even a bookstore in a hundred miles.

"Yeah, it just hit the stands. So much for trusting a journalist to respect 'off the record.' "

"She came right out and said you're a dyke?"

"No, I have to say that much for her. I guess she did respect my confidences. But she had so much other information from so many other sources that it's pretty clear to anybody reading between the lines that I'm queer." Hayley paused. "Unless somebody absolutely refuses to see it. Like the people who went to see *Fried Green Tomatoes* and thought the lead characters were just good friends. I thought Hollywood was over this shit, especially after *Go Fish*. We're supposed to be enjoying our 'Lesbian moment,' as Kate Clinton puts it."

I chuckled.

"Maybe it was me — my background isn't exactly role model lesbian. Anyway, the main money backed out. Richard Gere didn't, but he got a little queasy when he found out he was supposed to play the romantic lead that should have gone to a woman. He does look a little like you, though."

She giggled. My face was hot from finally hearing from her. And no one had ever compared me to Richard Gere before. I had to admit I enjoyed the comparison. At least our hair's the same, when he's not dying his for a role.

"It's funny, I can't help thinking that if I'd been upfront about being a lesbian from the start, I might have gotten the movie made anyway." Hayley's voice whined just a little. Self-pity is so unattractive in someone else.

"Maybe. Never can tell. Don't beat yourself up over your choices."

"Yeah, I'm doing a bit of that."

We might as well be talking about the weather, I thought. "So how the hell are you?" I finally asked.

"Good. I put on twenty pounds so I don't look like Kate Moss's 'Feed me' posters anymore. And yourself?"

"Fine. I'm fine, everybody's fine, the weather's fine too."

"Don't be upset, Laney. I know I haven't called. I just couldn't, that's all. But I'm feeling better now. I'd like to come see you. If you'll have me."

"If I'll have you!" What doubts?

"And by the way, I had my six-months HIV test. Still negative! My doctor says I can relax."

My mind reeled at those possibilities! No more dental dams, no more Saran wrap, no more K-Y

Jelly, no more surgical gloves and finger cots, no more condom-clad vibrators! Not that we hadn't managed quite well with those things while her status was uncertain, thank you.

She said she'd catch the United Express flight into the Ironwood airport tomorrow at four p.m. Thursday, December ninth.

I raced down to the kitchen and gave Tess and Kitt the news. They were delighted, in an abstract, disjointed sort of way. We ate the latkes and went back upstairs. Tess put the menorah in her window.

"You found lavender candles!" she said to Kitt. "Great!" She fingered the forty-eight four-inch tapers. In my direction she added, "The menorah is supposed to go in a window, as long as it's safe to do so."

"It's been so long. Let's see . . ." Kitt began. *"Baruch atah adonai . . ."*

"Hold on a minute." Tess lit one candle with a match. "The shamus," she said in my direction. "It's only used to light the rest of the candles." She used the shamus to light the taper farthest to the left. We watched it glow for a moment, sending a beam of golden light out into the snowy darkness. She whispered the Yiddish words and Kitt joined in here and there:

> *"Baruch atah adonai*
> *Eloheinu melech haolam*
> *Asher kidashanu bmitzvotav*
> *Vitzivanu l'hadlik ner*
> *Shel Hanukkah."*

To me, Tess said, "The traditional translation is,

'Blessed are you, my Lord, our God, king of the universe, who has commanded us to kindle the lights of Hanukkah.' But feminists usually do an interpretation." She smiled at Kitt. Her skin had a rosy glow, no more signs of the frostbite gray. "Maybe something like, Blessed are you, Sofia, Lilith, and our foremothers, who lead us unscathed through the patriarchy to discover our true female natures. May the lights of Hanukkah be a sign of our recommitment to our heritage. May our experience of being the only Jews in this area rekindle for us the strength of our community, just as the Maccabeans fought back against the assimilation ordered by the Syrian King Antiochus." She paused.

Kitt continued, "May this light be a symbol of our burning dedication to preserve our identity."

"And just as the Maccabeans used candles to rededicate the Temple after the desecrations of the Syrians, may these candles dedicate this hunting lodge to a new and higher spiritual purpose," Tess said.

I felt the urge to add something: "May this house and land become home to women's spirits running free, expressing ourselves in our own music and art." Kitt and Tess beamed at me, and then back at each other.

"Do you want to sing 'Maoz Tzur'?" Kitt said to Tess. "I think I remember it."

"Sure," Tess said, beginning the traditional song:

> "Rock of Ages, let our song
> Praise Thy saving power.
> Thou amidst the raging foes

Wast our shelt'ring tower.
Furious they assailed us
But Thine arm availed us,
    And Thy word
    Broke their sword
When our own strength failed us."

Kitt's alto voice rang loud, if not always on the same tune as Tess. I enjoyed watching the two of them. And Hayley was coming to me soon.

Kitt even had a dreydl in her suitcase, a gold toy top marked on each of its four sides with a Hebrew letter — N, G, H or *S*.

"The letters stand for the words *nimm, gib, halb* and *stell* — take, give, half and put," she explained to me. "It's a kid's game where you give or take nuts and other treats from your neighbor depending on which side the dreydl lands on." She spun the top and it fell over on the *N*.

"See, if we were playing now, I could take a nut from you, and then it would be your turn," Tess said, looking around for other little treats to use instead of nuts, but we felt foolish and stopped. We turned back to the menorah.

"Isn't there something about the significance of the eight candles, something about running out of oil?" I asked, watching the lavender candle burn low in the window.

Kitt explained that the Maccabeans thought they only had enough undefiled temple oil to last one night of the dedication ceremonies, but the tiny amount lasted the full eight days.

"The basic significance is more in the struggle of all cultural minorities to survive in a world that wants to do away with differences," Tess said. "I think this Hanukkah dedication can apply to the struggles of the lesbian community too. Thanks for adding your own blessing, Laney."

We talked quietly for at least an hour about current lesbian struggles and about our situation here at the lodge. This too was part of Hanukkah, Tess said. And then we offered thanks for whatever we felt like bringing up, as the candle sputtered and went out. I of course was thankful for Hayley's impending visit.

Neither Tess nor Kitt mentioned their fledgling relationship, maybe not wanting to take the chance of examining it too closely before it was full born. It soon became clear that I was the odd one out. I went to my own room and dreamed.

They didn't come down from Tess's room in the morning. I ate some Rice Krispies and a banana and left early for the airport. A State Police car drove up to the lodge as I was leaving, making rounds. It was only a twenty-mile drive to Gogebic County Airport, so I wasted time all day long in Ironwood, driving from store to store. I even ended up in Kmart, checking out shower curtains and VCRs.

Finally it was time. Despite four-wheel drive the Jeep slid on the icy road into the airport. I had my trusty emergency kit in the back, just in case I ended up in a ditch anyway.

We were to need the blankets from the kit almost immediately.

"Laney!" Hayley cried out before I spotted her.

She looked terrific, coming down the metal airplane stairs to the cleared cement apron. Her formerly shaved pale brown hair was a good two inches long now, trimmed into a pixie cut that accented her eyes. Maybe she'd added some blonde streaks, a reminder of her long tawny mane she'd had in her rock star days.

Her complexion said Michigan winter — pale and clear, a little pink-chapped on the cheekbones and lips. Something was different about her pale blue eyes, and then I realized they were encircled with mascara-laden lashes and gray-brown liner. She'd often complained how her eyes virtually disappeared when she had no tan for contrast, and unlike Angelenos, Michiganders don't have tans in December.

Hayley dropped her guitar case and her carry-on bag on the cement landing strip. She leaped off the last step from the commuter plane and into my arms. I reeled under the impact and our chapped faces and noses bumped until we got our lips together tight. The twelve-degree temperature soared between us.

I could almost hear letters to the editor being written all around us about those blatant L.A. lesbian intruders. We raced for the Jeep Cherokee through knee-high snow, like running a three-legged race in a feedsack. I pulled the car down the first cleared back road and we resumed our interrupted kiss while our hands wrestled feverishly with assorted buttons and straps. My ski jumpsuit had to go. Her authentic Navy peacoat hit the floor.

The periwinkle of a deep-yoked pirate's shirt, worn over faded jeans, loaned her eyes more color. That full-breasted figure, which had been the launching pad to her teenage career as much as her voice, was even more sensational now that she was, what, forty-three?

At five p.m. in mid-December, deep in an Upper Peninsula Michigan white pine forest, it was already dark, though the snow glowed. The car windows steamed over immediately. I put on the heat for a moment, but since it seemed likely we were going to be staying right there for a while, I turned off the engine to avoid asphyxiation. We were making our own heat.

A half-Nelson landed us both in the back seat. A full Nelson flopped us into the luggage area, butting heads against the wall-mount spare tire and Hayley's guitar case and suitcase. Our shirts remained in the front seat, our jeans were somewhere in the middle, underwear was missing in action. We made an igloo out of the white chenille blankets from my car's emergency kit. The snow began to make an igloo out of the Cherokee.

So this is what she tasted like, minus the piña colada dental dams and the patchouli oils and the chocolate syrup and Cool Whip. I dove into her with my tongue. I settled onto her magic button and let my fingers sink deep into her wetness. She held her own nipples and laughed aloud in delight as if I were tickling her, her teeth chattering and goosebumps erupting on her arms and legs.

Was she shivering or orgasming? A bit of both. A lot of both. She shook and I held her, gasping, coming up for air and seeking her mouth, melding tastes together. Hayley was back.

CHAPTER EIGHTEEN

I'd seen a motel a few miles from the airport. "We're going to freeze to death if we stay here," I said, getting the words out between kisses. "Let me go, just for a second."

I struggled to find all my clothes and gave up, making my way to the front seat and sliding my way naked into the discarded, now ice-cold, jumpsuit.

"You can stay back there under the blankets if you want — I'm finding us someplace to spend the night. I can't make it back to the lodge."

Dragging one of the white blankets around her, she lunged over the seats and into my lap, setting off the horn. The blare may have startled a raccoon or deer, but there were no humans within hearing range. I relented and took her back in my arms, fighting with the steering wheel for space.

Her kisses made me forget about the snow, the plunging temperatures, the possibility of a car or snowplow coming down this road. The heat between us made such scenarios seem implausible at best.

Sweat pooled in my jumpsuit. I started to take it off again, when my elbow hit the window and I jumped at the icy touch. Since rescuing Tess, my skin was still supersensitive to cold. "Please, we've got to get out of here and into someplace warm," I said.

"So do it," she said, tugging the zipper of my jumpsuit farther south. I reached for the gearshift and she buried her head in my belly, trying unsuccessfully to reach my clit with her mouth. She settled for my nipples instead, letting her hands roam between my legs. How do you drive in a situation like this? Very carefully. I moved the car forward a few inches.

Her fingers found my most perfect place, a quarter inch above and to the right of my hooded hot spot. She was careful not to rub too hard or too directly, teasing me, testing her placement. Yes, she had it right.

She was relentless. I couldn't drive. I couldn't do anything but turn off the ignition once more. My nipples were caressed and licked and manipulated till they were super-charged. Her fingers kneaded me.

Her massage took me into another world, far from

the icebox we were in, a world as I imagined Tahiti to be. I let myself float in the warm tide as my body responded. She took me all the way to Tahiti.

I was slumped over the steering wheel, the horn blaring again, when I realized where we really were. "Come on, I've got to get us to a motel," I insisted.

She didn't resist this time, turning the dashboard heat up to high before climbing back over the seats to get her clothes. Once dressed, she sat on her side in silence, merely giving me an enigmatic smile, enjoying me, devouring me with her eyes. I felt very, very loved.

"I love you, Hayley," I said.

"I love you too."

There, we'd said it. Everything was all right again. No doubts.

At the motel we made love all night and collapsed from exhaustion in the morning. Check-out time was one in the afternoon; we were gathering our clothes as the housekeeper was turning the key in our door. I treated Hayley to lunch at the Liberty Bell Chalet and drove her around the area, which didn't take long.

We did spend some time along Lake Superior, listening to the sounds of ice shards building up along the coastline only to be crushed by each incoming splashing wave. Soaring seagulls called to us for handouts. A loon chortled its lunatic laugh. The sky was like the coat of a dappled gray Appaloosa, tufts of dark clouds sailing across a milk bath, occasional snowflakes glistening white on white. We drove to the Black River and hiked through the leafless woods through the snow, back toward one of the river's seven waterfalls, following the birch log railing that indicated a State Parks trail. At the clearing at the end of the trail, we watched the build-up of an ice palace made of frozen droplets. And we kissed again, and hugged, and contemplated doing it in the snow before our brains took hold once more. We half-ran, half-crashed through the snow getting back to the car, shivering all the way.

"I'm ready to see this hunting lodge," Hayley said. "I hope it has a fireplace."

"Dozens of them," I assured her. I started to tell her all about the lodge when I realized I hadn't said anything about the accident that had happened only two days ago. It felt like years.

"Here we go again," she said with a forlorn sigh when I'd completed the story. "I thought I was recovered. I thought I'd gotten my life back, and here we go, back into a situation where I don't know what's going to happen next. I don't think I can handle it." Her face, which had been so alive, was ashen.

"I should have told you on the phone," I said. "I didn't think. All I could think of was seeing you. Do you want me to drive you back to the airport? Back to your brother's?"

She thought a long time, her pale eyes flickering. "The cops are in on this already, right? They have three or four suspects and they're checking them out, so they should have an answer soon?"

"Right. The state trooper in charge impresses me a lot, though he has his moments like any other cop I've ever met. Guess it's the job." I told her about the tests that were run on the drops of motor oil found at the lake. She couldn't believe my description of Gerlock's not-so-hermitlike computer headquarters out in the middle of nowhere. Gradually she relaxed. It helped when she saw a police car making its rounds on the lodge's back roads as we drove up. The officer waved at me as he passed.

"Moment of decision. Do you want to go inside, or do you want me to drive you back to the airport?"

"We're here. I might as well see what the lodge is like and talk to Kitt and this Tess person. You really think she'd showcase me in this music festival thing?"

"She'd be thrilled to have you," I said. I noticed that Tess's Blazer was gone. "She must be showing Kitt around town, or they've gone to the store or something. You can meet them later. Come on in to my humble abode."

Hayley was properly impressed by the lodge, oohing and aahing over each new room as I presented the possibilities. I took her up to my room and she dumped her suitcases on my bed and plopped herself down. Before I could join her, a flutter of yellow on my door caught my eye.

"What's this?" One of Kitt's notorious Post-it notes was stuck on my door at eye level:

"We flew back to Los Angeles. I'll call you.
Kitt."

Her handwriting is so bad that Kitt usually prints, as she had done here. "That's strange," I said. "They hadn't said anything about leaving so soon."

"Umm," Hayley said. "I really wanted to meet this Tess. You said Kitt was only going to stay a few days and Tess might leave as early as the fifteenth. So they decided to go early? Maybe they didn't like the feel of this scene either. If I were Tess I'd be scared silly. Maybe we should go back too."

"Do you want me to take you back to the airport?" I asked again. I resisted kissing her, not wanting to exert undue influence on her to stay. Part of me wanted to rush right to the airport and the sanity of L.A. — hah, wasn't that a strange thought. But I was in full gear now — Hayley and I had more business to take care of, now that we were back in warmth.

Instead of taking me up on my offer, she stood up and kissed me, then pulled me back onto the bed on top of her, on top of her suitcase and guitar case. We rolled around on the lumps and maneuvered the luggage onto the floor while we struggled out of our clothes once more. We didn't come up for air until dusk had settled over the lodge and the room had gone dark. I turned on the lights as I headed for the bathroom. Hayley joined me in the shower. A lost weekend of the very best kind.

It was around four a.m. when I awoke from a nightmare about noisy snowmobiles zooming around me like killer bees. Hayley slept soundly. I got out of bed and sat on the windowseat overlooking the peaceful white landscape and watched snowflakes twinkle in the moonlight.

Something was nagging at me, something about the note from Kitt. It hit me. No one from L.A. says the whole words "Los Angeles," only the abbreviation.

And Kitt wouldn't say she'd call me. She uses her e-mail or fax every time she can. She'd say something like, "Check your e-mail." Kitt usually prints, but the letters were pressed in a little harder than usual, now that I thought about it. And the line crossing the double "t" was too short. She kind of drags it out.

But then maybe she was writing the note in a rush. And who's to say an Angeleno might not write out "Los Angeles" once in a while? I squirmed on the windowseat and stared into the night.

Something below caught my eye. I thought I saw two shadowy figures walking rapidly away from the lodge and toward the road. I froze and went to the phone and called Detective Lamppa's direct line to his home.

"I'll have a car scouting the property in minutes," he said, sleep leaving his voice as he spoke. "Are you absolutely sure you saw two people?"

"I think so. It's dark and they were dressed in dark clothes."

"They were probably our men, checking the property."

"I don't think so. These men were ... skulking."

"Okay, we'll check it out. Go back to sleep. The officers will wake you at the lodge if they find something. I'll come by myself first thing in the morning."

"Thanks, Detective. We'll be all right."

No way could I sleep. Where did that door lead to? Hadn't the interior decorator's assistant said something seemed a little off in the room measurements? Tess had taken a FedEx delivery, I remembered — maybe the architectural plans we'd ordered from Chicago. My master key fit her room.

The bed didn't look slept in. Kitt had brought one large suitcase, and it was gone, but Tess's green soft-siders were still in the back of the closet. None of her clothes seemed to be missing.

I pulled out one of a half-dozen loose, drop-waisted jumpers jammed into one end of the closet. If she'd gone back to L.A., for sure she'd have taken her jumpers with her. I saw her wear nothing else while she was there. Her ballerina flats were on the floor. So were her cowboy boots and ski boots and Bass Weejuns; only a pair of slippers seemed to be missing.

"Strange," I said aloud. The hairs on the back of my neck were tickling. I looked through her drawers and found the layouts.

There it was, an extension of the basement beyond the fuel tank room. I didn't remember any doors behind the tanks that would lead to that area. And the high-pointed roof that supposedly served only to keep snow from accumulating also hid a huge attic with storage shelves. But the only way into the attic was from a staircase that began in the hidden basement section.

Puzzled, I looked around Tess's empty room for anything else that looked suspicious. Then I spotted it. A hundred blue-green ceramic pieces in the wastebasket. Kitt's prized menorah. The oval shape of the menorah's base could be seen in the faint dust on the sill.

Maybe a draft blew through the window, or the curtain caught on it, I told myself. It's ceramic, after all — it would break easily.

But into that many pieces? It had to have been hurled with tremendous force. Had Tess and Kitt had a fight? Neither of them seemed the type to throw things in an argument, certainly not a menorah.

I picked up the closest phone in Tess's suite. No dial tone again. I panicked.

"What's up?"

Hayley's voice from the hall gave me a start. "Something's very wrong," I said. "I'm getting us out of here and into a motel. Hurry!"

To get her moving I told her of the people I'd seen last night, and my suspicions about a hidden basement room to the lodge.

"I can't help feeling that Kitt and Tess are still at the lodge," I finally admitted as I got us into the Jeep.

Hayley's face registered fear only briefly before a peaceful smile returned.

Where to go? All I could think of was the out-of-the-way motel Hayley and I had spent the blissful night before.

As I drove, glancing over at Hayley when I could, I saw her slip back into the catatonic state I'd seen so often when we were dealing with her supposed "ghost" during the summer. Her eyes lost their focus, her shoulders slumped, her jaw went slack. I was in shock myself, over her transformation as well as over the implications of being under siege again. I couldn't think about how to handle her transition now. All I could concentrate on was that she'd be no help in this crisis. I'd have to think this through myself.

CHAPTER NINETEEN

By the time I got Hayley to Ironwood it was dawn. To her it was as if nothing had happened; she was in a state of total denial. It was easiest to go along with her and not force her to speed up. She was hungry and wanted a leisurely sit-down meal. We drove through Burger King — I got extra food so that we wouldn't have to leave the motel while I figured out what to do.

Part of me wanted to stay at the motel with Hayley in safety, while another part was drawn to the trouble at the lodge. I turned on the television and finally settled on CNN, thinking that some hard news might help me get centered again with a little reality check on the world. Hayley seemed placid enough, getting her guitar out of its case and strumming to herself. Songs from the sixties.

"Get some more sleep if you can," I told her. "I'm going to go back to the lodge and meet with Lammpa." At last I'd have her off my hands. One less worry. She put down the guitar and stared with zombie eyes toward the television.

"Hold me," she said. "Please."

I sat down next to her on the bed and rubbed her back. We watched the news wrap-up together. Eventually we both fell asleep. When I awoke CNN was on yet another wrap-up of the news.

There on the screen was a picture of the Tessel Hunting and Fishing Lodge! What was it doing on TV? I turned up the volume and learned that the shot instead was of the Lake Michigan Conference Center.

The voice-over said that the building was going to be the site of a major "think tank" summit conference on the growing neo-Nazi movement in the U.S. in early January. Hundreds of Jewish leaders and representatives of all the major liberal organizations were going to be at the conference, which had grown out of the memorials to the fifty-year anniversary of the Holocaust.

"It could happen again," a rabbi said into a microphone. "We're going to make sure it doesn't."

My entire body went into a shiver. I turned off the television. Hayley's eyes were closed. I hoped she stayed asleep. Ideas that had swirled through my dreams all night like a kaleidoscope now came to a halt in one horrifying montage. I had to get back to the lodge. But first, at a pay phone outside the motel, I made a call.

Before driving back to the lodge, I went to Camp Tessel. Too many clues pointed to Hank Gerlock. Sure, he was nice, overly nice. But the fact remained that his business card had the number of a bulletin board service currently filled with anti-Semitic venom. His library of guerrilla warfare books and tapes had been unsettling, not to mention the fact that Camp Tessel itself bordered on paramilitarism.

Now to find that Tess's lodge had the same layout as an Illinois hotel that was hosting a conference on neo-Nazism that would draw many outstanding Jewish activists? And Kitt and Tess were still missing, and I'd seen men going into a hidden basement section of the lodge, and the state police still weren't taking it seriously. I had to act myself, despite my terror.

No cars were in the parking lot at Camp Tessel when I drove by. I parked out of sight from the road and made my way to the garage. No sign of a Land Rover or any other vehicle.

Dusk comes early to Michigan in December. Luckily I'd grabbed my warmest outfit, the black ski suit with the blue pin stripes, which should blend in with the shadowed trees. All I needed was a black ski mask, but my jumpsuit hood camouflaged most of my head.

I squeezed through the fence at the gate to look around. Gerlock was nowhere to be found. No sign of anyone, anywhere. He could be at another seminar in Chicago, maybe with that Angelique creature, or anyplace. But I was sure he was with Tess and Kitt, wherever they might be.

I went to the cabin that served as a store and rammed the door with all of my weight. How come police officers on TV knock down doors with almost no effort? My shoulder hurt from repeated impacts. Finally the door gave, the jamb in splinters. I took two semi-automatic pistols and ammo and jammed them inside my jumpsuit into my jeans waistband and went back to my car. At least I would look armed.

Near the lodge, I hid the Jeep around a curve down a side road and hiked in on the secondary roads toward the main building. I didn't have on quite so many layers of clothes as when we'd gone snowmobiling, and I missed them, but my fast pace kept me warm.

As I neared the garage from the far side of the main building I heard a car approaching and hid behind a tree. The minivan drove up to the garage and parked close to the rear wall. It was Rudy's navy Suburban. He was one of the two people who got out and walked toward the rear of the lodge — I could tell it was him by the way he overcompensated for his slight limp from what I'd guessed earlier was an arthritic hip.

The other figure was tall, probably a man close to my height. As Gerlock was. I couldn't see their faces; they'd remembered their masks. They drew a voluminous tarp over the van in such a way that it might be mistaken for a covered woodpile or a snowplow. I followed the men, moving quickly from tree to tree, as they made their way toward the lodge. They talked animatedly, heatedly, but I couldn't hear the words.

No wonder I'd never seen the door. The men stopped at one of the outside stone chimneys and lifted a fake stone to reveal a keyhole. Rudy inserted a key and the stone-covered door swung open. They went inside.

I took a deep breath and darted to the door and found it was slightly ajar. A tug on the stone edge and it opened enough for me to look through the crack.

There was a corridor, lined with several dark rooms with no doors, and one brightly lit room at the end of the corridor where voices could be heard. I could hide in one of the other rooms. I slipped inside and into the first dark room. When my eyes adjusted I could see it was full of big wooden crates stacked ceiling-high. The tops were nailed shut.

I still couldn't hear any specific words from this room, though a full-fledged shouting match was underway, and so I peeked into the corridor. No one was in sight. I ducked into the next room. One of the crates here was open.

Guns. Stuff that looked like the night vision binoculars and other equipment that the news clips kept showing during Desert Storm. Camouflage uniforms. Some of the guns looked like rocket launchers, but I couldn't tell. All I knew was that I was in shock, almost paralyzed in fear. What had I found? What was I going to do about it?

From this room the words became distinct.

"... we'd never be in this position. How are we going to get out of this mess, did you ever think of that?"

"I just couldn't kill them!" Rudy's voice whined. "I didn't mind trying to make Tess's life miserable all summer, trying to make her get sick of the joint and sell it off. The Foundation would make the highest offer, and then you'd have what you wanted, all the land reunited again. I did a good job, didn't I?" He was pleading.

"You scared her, all right. She went off to California and brought back another one! And now they just keep coming! We're going to have to leave the country once the training ends. And we had such a good thing going here."

I heard a shoving sound.

"You got your orders. And you failed. How could you have missed?"

The other voice rose to a shout. It had to be Gerlock. There was a blunt sound and a groan.

"I told you, no one could have traced the bullets to you. You had sabot sheaths for the shells, absolutely untraceable."

Now I could detect the slight German accent. Another sound, like a slap.

"I just couldn't kill them!" Rudy wailed.

"And then you messed up with the snowmobile trails," the other voice sneered. "Such a simple thing. They go over the lake by mistake and fall in, never to be found until spring."

"It's not my fault one lagged behind and then rescued the other." Rudy sniffled.

"I had to act so nice to the Juden, taking them to the hospital, paying their bills, to keep their attention off of me," the voice said.

This was one time I wished I hadn't been right.

"I should have shot them on sight and dragged their bodies back to the lake. But instead, I had to come up with something else, thanks to your failure, you sniveling idiot."

Another thud, another groan.

"And now we've got four bitches to deal with. We're going to have to kill all four. Why couldn't you have done your job in the first place?"

A kicking sound.

"And then when you go up to their room to retrieve the bug you smash their menorah! Don't you think somebody might put two and two together soon?"

"I don't know, I ... I looked up and saw that Jewish candle thing shining in the window and I just ... lost it."

"Asshole!" The sound of a kick and a groan. "You lost it all right, you may have cost me the whole thing, you fuck-up. The clock is ticking. Our training starts in two days. We have to deal with these women without arousing any suspicion, or all our plans fail."

A flurry of sounds. I backed farther into the darkened room. This one was full of cardboard cartons. Apparently these boxes held flyers and pamphlets; samples of the contents of each box were on top. I ripped one booklet loose — *The International Jew*, the title read, and I could see a photograph and the signature of Henry Ford on the cover. I crammed it inside my waistband. Up against the two guns.

The two men left. I stayed behind the boxes until I heard the outside door make a heavy thud.

"Kitt! Tess! I'm here!" I dashed into the lit room and found them tied to wooden chairs, gray duct tape over their mouths. I got the tape off first and they both were talking so fast I couldn't distinguish what they were saying. "Stay still a second, I can't get these knots loose," I said. No knife in sight. I worked feverishly to free them.

"Thank God you're here." Tess sobbed. "Rudy got me when I went downstairs to make breakfast yesterday, and he got Kitt when she came down looking for me. He hit me on the head with a rolling pin and before I could recover I was taped up and herded into this room." She motioned toward a wooden door at the far end of the lit room. "There's another hidden door to this place from the rear of the fuel oil room." I checked quickly. It was locked. No escape that route.

"Hank is a madman who thinks World War Two never ended and the second coming of Hitler is upon us," Kitt said. "Rudy served in the SS during World War II. They kept calling us *Juden.*"

When her hands were freed Kitt rubbed her cheeks and the back of her neck and then her wrists. Her hair was plastered to her head with nervous sweat that also dripped down her flushed face. "They said they're planning a guerrilla training session here next week to prepare to attack some conference in Chicago in January. Apparently a lot of Jews are going to be there. Something about neo-Nazism."

I told them briefly about the CNN spot I'd seen.

211

"We'll talk later. We've got to figure out how to get out of here alive. They plan to kill us. They had your room bugged, maybe this one is too."

"It wouldn't need to be — they're the only ones who know about it," Tess cut in. "They can turn everything in the lodge off and on from here. The only reason we had electricity left on upstairs is that they need it down here and somehow the circuits are linked." I wrestled with the ropes binding her slipper-clad feet.

I glanced around and saw a heavy compact cube electric space heater, microwave, refrigerator, a twin bed with bare mattress piled with comforters, television and radio, wooden chairs and Formica table, and a rust-stained toilet and sink. All the comforts of home.

"Gerlock's using his computers for the communications link-ups," Kitt said. "Rudy has been here most of the time, but Gerlock is the brains and the link to all these groups. I heard about this stuff on 'Sixty Minutes' but I never dreamed it was real."

I heard sounds from outside. A car pulling up in front of the lodge. "Quick, someone's here, you'll have to finish untying yourselves. Here, take these guns. If they come back, aim for their eyes."

Kitt and Tess stared at me.

"Paintball guns, that's all I could find. See what else you can use as weapons. Throw that space heater at them. Cans of food, anything you can find. We have to catch them off guard long enough to grab their guns. The real ones."

I ran out of the room and down the corridor toward the outer stone-faced door. I planned to peek outside and decide whether to hide in one of the other rooms or sneak out.

My decision was made for me. The door swung open. There was Detective Cyprian Lamppa in uniform.

I felt a wave of relief. "Thank God you're here!"

Then I saw that Rudy and Hank were right behind him.

All three men entered the stone door, so that we had a face-off in the dark corridor. And then Lamppa turned and shot Rudy in the chest.

The old man slumped to the floor, blood oozing out from under his body. He let out a groan and was silent. It was obvious he was dead.

"What did you do that for?" I shouted without thinking.

"He just killed you four girls, and I had to shoot him in the line of duty," Cyprian grinned wickedly. "That solution answers all our problems."

"You stupid . . . !" Gerlock was livid beyond words, his whole body twitching as if he'd touched a live wire. He visibly forced himself back under control. "You think the cops are going to simply take your word for how the murders took place and go away? They'll be swarming over this building for weeks, and our people start arriving in two days!"

Gerlock's mouth tightened in a grimace. "What's done is done. Now we need to hide the bodies until we're through. Someplace where they won't smell."

"Bury them in a snowbank."

"Some snowmobiler might take a shortcut and land on top of them, or some animal might drag a half-eaten arm onto the road. No . . . I've got it. We'll string 'em up on hooks in the food locker. That should please Tess the gourmet. All we need is a week and we're out of here. I've drained the Foundation dry. We can hide out forever. But first we have a job to do." He leered at me.

"Get in there with your friends," Lamppa said, pushing me toward the lit room. Gerlock followed us.

"What . . ." The empty chairs unnerved Lamppa for the split-second Tess and Kitt needed. They were hidden on either side of the entrance and jumped out behind the men.

As the men spun around, Kitt and Tess shot as ordered at the men's faces. Drops of red flew everywhere, covering the men's faces, getting into their eyes. Lamppa staggered, and momentarily his hand dropped. I kicked with all the force in me and knocked his gun loose. It skidded down the hall and bounced off a wall into one of the other rooms.

"Ow, ow, ow," Hank yelped. "Hey, this is paint!" He scrubbed at his face, trying to see, his eyes blinded, his mouth in a furious tight line. Before his hand could get inside his coat, Tess conked him in the temple with the space heater. He slid to the floor. Tess dug for his gun and threw it behind her. It slid under the bed.

From the corner of my eye I could see she was now beating him with a chair. It fell apart and she kept using one chair leg on him like a baseball bat. He grabbed it from her momentarily and she leapt on his chest, her knees sending some two hundred pounds into his sternum. He groaned and fell back, enough time for her to wrench the chair leg away and go at it again.

Lamppa got me by my elbow, his other hand still

scrubbing at his eyes, not sure which one of us he had, but he was going to break my arm any second. I kicked in the direction of his groin in futility as he twisted my hand behind me so tightly I expected to hear the bones snap. With my free hand I poked into his eye sockets.

Kitt rammed the palm of her hand hard against the tip of his nose, ramming the nose bone into his brain.

"Ow!" He screamed and let go of me to grab his face. He reeled from the impact. This time I did get his groin with my foot. He bent over. Between repeated attacks on Gerlock with the chair leg, Tess gave Lamppa his share as well. Both men appeared to sink into unconsciousness.

"Quick, get them tied up good," I said. "Use that duct tape all over the bastards."

In the movies, if a woman actually does knock out a bad guy, she drags herself away and forgets about him, and he comes to and grabs her again, to get double suspense out of a scene. I wasn't going to make that stupid mistake. From the way Tess was getting off walloping both the men with that chair leg, neither was she. I pulled her off of them and retrieved both guns. I wedged them in my waistband, feeling like the star of a western shootout. Their hard metal barrels rubbed against my groin — no wonder the guys like these things.

"Don't kill the bastards, let them suffer some more," I told Tess. "Like life in prison." Reluctantly she put down her makeshift bat.

"What were those knots I learned in Girl Scouts?" Kitt grinned as she straightened out the rope to use on her former captors.

And then we all heard the sounds outside, like an Indy Five Hundred race was about to crash through the door. Male war whoops, an army of them. A whole battalion of clamoring tanks, just outside, getting closer. Roars and shouts.

Kitt, Tess and I rushed outside, trying to figure out what was happening. We stood in the doorway, peering into the trees.

We were hit from behind and sent sprawling to the floor. Lamppa and Gerlock rushed outdoors for freedom.

Four or five snowmobiles roared in circles and figure eights in the yard. The two men on foot were surrounded. When one of the machines got close to me, I could hear over the noise a woman's voice shouting: "Don't let them get away!"

"Hayley!" I screamed.

She was holding tight behind a man in a black leather motorcycle jacket who seemed to be the leader of this army, crouching in the seat of his white snowmobile like Willie Shoemaker riding a stallion to victory. The Highwaymen on Arctic Cats. They were having a high old time. Hayley waved a bottle in the air and yelled like a cheerleader, apparently urging the men onward, though I couldn't hear the words.

When her ride circled close again, she yelled, "These are the guys, right?" I nodded, shocked speechless. "So run 'em down, boys." She gave the order like a gangster moll, the rest of her words drowned out again by the engines' roars.

All of them were drunk. The men on snowmobiles aimed at the escaping Gerlock and Lamppa, pelting them with beer bottles once they'd taken their last swigs. They made their machines sideswipe and bump

216

the running men until Gerlock and Lamppa fell on their faces into the snow.

"Don't kill 'em, just stop 'em," Hayley's voice rang clear. The snowmobiles slowed to wide circles and stopped. The four riders plus Hayley staggered off their machines and toward me, since Hayley was acknowledging me as the center of authority in this scene.

I was still unable to speak, my throat constricted to the point that cackling sounds came out instead of words. "Think deep, roar from your chest, or you'll never be able to shout for help," I remembered from a rape self-defense class. I tried to breathe deeply. I'd forgotten we were outside in near-zero weather; my chest caught fire. And my bruises from the fight were starting to make themselves felt.

"Okay, there's rope and tape in the room at the end of the corridor, inside that stone door that's swinging open," Kitt said, recovering more quickly, though she too kept rubbing her head and back. "If you guys would do us the favor of tying these two up so tight even Houdini couldn't get loose, we'll be eternally grateful."

"Hey, the fuzz, too?" one snowmobiler asked, looking more closely at Lamppa's prone body as the officer groaned and writhed in pain.

"He's one of the bad guys," I replied, finally able to talk.

The snowmobiler gave me a wide grin. "Hey, this is fun! I always wanted to tie up a cop." He looked at Hayley again. "You sure this is right?"

"I told you, damsels in distress. These are my friends." She gave a sloppy wave that encompassed all of us. "And those two were kidnapped," Hayley pointed at Tess and Kitt. "Hey, we really did rescue them, just like I said!" She looked astonished, as if suddenly realizing what had happened.

"Hayley, you're drunk," I said.

"Yeah, I am, and what are you going to do about it?" She could barely hold her belligerent stance.

Nothing.

Kitt and Tess and I made sure the men tied Gerlock and Lamppa securely. Tess wanted to belt them a few more times but we assured her that they would get their just rewards.

The phones were working again. I made a follow-up call, adding my new information.

I walked outside and told the group that the FBI was on its way. Their closest agent in Duluth should be arriving any moment with plenty of help.

The man who'd said he'd always wanted to tie up a cop reacted to the news by jumping back on his snowmobile. "Let's split this scene," he said to the others. The noisy machines tore into the trails.

"Where did you pick up those guys?" I asked Hayley when the noise had faded to the point she could hear me.

"Hey, weren't they great?"

"We had the situation under control when you guys came in like the cavalry. Okay, I'm glad you brought them. But how did you get them?"

"Oh, I waited around for you and never heard any more, so I figured you were in trouble. I didn't feel any too good, so I went to the bar next door."

Now was not the time for an AA lecture.

"There were these guys who were out for a ride

on their snowmobiles and they'd stopped for a drink or two, and we got to talking." Hayley finally looked at me and could see that I was not as enthused about her rescue attempt as she'd expected. Of course, if things had gone a little differently, I might have had to be a whole lot more grateful.

Hayley rambled on, glancing at me with alternate defiance and sheepishness. "Pretty soon I told them the whole story and they got all excited and said they had to come rescue the damsels in distress. And here we are. Or were."

She shuffled around as if the liquor wasn't quite in control anymore. She looked at the bottle, a cheap scotch, and threw it into the woods. She tried to meet my eyes again and couldn't.

"At least it wasn't cherry wine," she muttered, mostly to herself.

There were no words for all I wanted to say, but this was not the time or place. Fury, disgust, pity . . . "We'll talk later," I said, trying to keep my voice even. I turned away from her.

Now that the crisis was over, or at least settled for now, I could feel how cold it was. Except for Hayley, the rest of us were shivering. "We'd better get inside," I said. "Especially you, Tess. Your skin isn't recovered from the last time."

"What do we do with these jerks?" Kitt asked.

"Let them get frostbite. It's the least we can do." But we dragged their roped and taped bodies by their feet, their heads tunneling through the snow, to the front porch and left them there with a little protection from the wind and cold. Even powerless to get their hands and legs free, the men kicked and thrust their bodies like inch worms making their convoluted way.

"Don't hurt the furniture," Tess told them as we went inside. "Feel free to hurt yourselves."

I did go back to the hidden rooms and check on Rudy. There was no pulse, no breathing. I left him as he was.

The first round of FBI personnel arrived half an hour later, accompanied by state troopers from another county, while three of us were warming ourselves in front of the fireplace. Hayley was upstairs in my room, alone with her thoughts. She'd said she didn't feel well, and I was sure she didn't.

These officers were prepared to take us seriously, after directives from on high, and they took notes and tape-recorded our stories before taking Hank and Cyprian away in their patrol cars. They strung yellow plastic streamers around much of the yard and the basement. They called the county coroner to take Rudy's body and a crime scene specialist to examine the hidden rooms.

We repeated our stories for these experts when they arrived a few hours later, at early dawn, and found us half-sleeping on the corduroy sofa in the living room with remnants of sandwiches that had served as lunch and dinner.

Apparently the FBI was at work throughout the country, pulling together information from many undercover sources relating to the upcoming conference on neo-Nazism. "We want to get these guys, all of them," one agent, Paul Cochetti, told us. "We have an idea."

* * * * *

And so a gigantic sting was set up, with an officer who looked a lot like Gerlock put in place to greet the terrorists coming to the lodge for the training session. They were nabbed quietly one by one over the next week, while Tess, Kitt, Hayley and I remained invisible inside the lodge. Clockwork.

When the stream of arrivals had ended and we could be seen in public again, I drove Hayley to the Ironwood airport. Her brother's wife said she would meet Hayley at Detroit Metro.

It was time to tell the world about this latest show of force by the neo-Nazi movement, which would have taken it into new heights of terrorism. One of the FBI's media relations staff, Mackey Fields, arrived to take charge of this phase of the operations.

He set up a press conference for one p.m., enough time for Detroit and Chicago media to make it to the U.P., plenty of time for the camera crews to get back for the five o'clock news shows. Beyond making sure that the FBI received full credit for the successful operation, Mackey turned the interviews over to us. "We like to be low key, ma'am," he said.

At fifty, I guess I should expect "ma'am." It's a step up from "Miss" and "girl." He meant no harm.

I insisted that Wanda Krakabowski be given the chance to write the first story, which went over the Associated Press newswire out of the Ironwood *Globe*. This could be her big chance, and I wanted to pay her back for helping my investigation. I gave her the basic information by phone, promising a more in-depth story later. She wrote up a few pages, enough

221

to draw every reporter and film crew who could make it to the U.P. You'd have thought a new Gold Rush was on. The cars and vans crossing the Mackinac Bridge must have looked like the O.J. Simpson chase.

The television crews had a ball, wandering through the lodge, filming the moose mascot and the luxury rooms and the lake where Tess's snowmobile went through the ice. They "accidentally" broke through the yellow police lines and got scolded like naughty youngsters by officers. It was almost great fun for all of them, a novelty. Not the exhausting weariness of an L.A. crime scene where everyone has seen too much already in their lives.

Crews filmed FBI trucks hauling away box after box of the weapons and propaganda from the lodge's basement and attic. Tess was told that she'd get all the brochures back after the trial, if she wanted. She grimaced at the thought. Next, photographers filmed me reading aloud the most disgusting parts of *The International Jew*. I brought up Gerlock's bulletin board service on my computer and let the cameras pan for themselves over the semi-literate anti-Semitism still flaming over the wires.

When we gathered around the TV to see ourselves on the news, I was surprised to see myself getting the most air time. Reporters had talked to all of us, and I had tried to explain the story as succinctly as possible. Everyone else must have rambled, the first cardinal sin of news interviews.

Meanwhile, the first cardinal sin of public relations is to get the media attention on yourself rather than on your client, but Tess insisted that she didn't want to speak to the media anymore. "I'm perfectly happy to let you hog the cameras," she said, grinning.

"And you, Kitt? You're the boss. Do you want to do the rest of the interviews?"

"You take the publicity," Kitt agreed. "I just got here. You're the one who figured out what happened. You're the only one who knows the whole story."

She cocked her head at me. "Besides, this kind of publicity wouldn't be that great for Meyers Music. Somebody getting half the story might think we were mixed up in this somehow and shy away from anything controversial."

She was right, I agreed.

"All I need is for someone to hear the tail end of the news, get it all garbled, and decide Kitt Meyers is anti-Semitic! Carry on, Laney!"

So I repeated myself to the media for hours on end, that evening and the next few days, trying to remain fresh for each new interview. Kitt found throat lozenges for me in Tess's medicine chest and made fresh pots of coffee. We ate the FBI's doughnuts, brought in for the press conference, between tapings.

Finally all the reporters were out of the house and the satellite transmitter TV vans were gone. Kitt, Tess and I sat in front of the fireplace and talked quietly, trying to figure everything out, trying to come to terms with what had happened.

CHAPTER TWENTY

The focus of most news stories moved on to interviews with the experts on neo-Nazism who were to speak at the Chicago conference, and to whichever neo-Nazi spokespersons could be persuaded to respond.

A few agents from the Federal Bureau of Investigation and Alcohol, Tobacco and Firearms stayed around to see what else might be uncovered. An FBI agent gave me a copy of *Soldier of Fortune* and *The Survivalist* magazines to show me the coded advertisements that led people to find each other and hate groups.

Gerlock had an open advertisement for his paintball programs, a quarter page of sophistry making Camp Tessel seem like a Boy Scout summer camp. Family values indeed.

More frightening was a blatant advertisement for "The Israeli Challenge Training Program," featuring such sessions as sharp shooting, hand-to-hand combat Israeli Commando style, anti-terrorist and hostage crisis, covert operations, emergency war medical training, and a "Bedouin Dinner Experience in the Judean Desert." All tours would be in "deluxe air-conditioned motor coaches" — so much for total guerrilla living.

The ad proclaimed, "All instructors are former elite Israeli Commandos and fluent in English." Cost was $3,100 per person, group discounts available. Besides a phone number, there was an Internet e-mail number via Compuserve. The educational institution offering this experience called itself "The Israeli Sky Connection Ltd."

I also saw advertisements for the various books and videotapes I'd seen in Gerlock's computer room, and more that made me even sicker. Hitler still lives, at least in the hearts of haters everywhere.

One thing further investigations uncovered was an antique but working printing press, also lodged in the basement. I'm having an expert come out in the spring to see if it is suitable for use by the authors who will come to Tess's lodge to write. Maybe some of them will be able to self-publish their works, or, if the equipment is still good enough, she might end up with her own small press!

Lamppa couldn't wait to turn state's evidence against Gerlock, hoping for a reduced sentence on the murder charge; neither had any sort of prior record. He was the only state trooper involved in Gerlock's operations, which was a great relief to the people of Beer Barrel and Ironwood.

Making himself at home with a cup of Tess's strong coffee, the agent proceeded to drone on about hate groups, though I actually found it fascinating.

One of the FBI agents verified that there was a possible link between the car bomber caught in New York, Gerlock and Tess. Gerlock had done a smooth job embezzling from the Foundation, and all financial records were apparently under scrutiny.

After the sixties, apparently, the Klan evolved into a couple of very large competing organizations which were highly disorganized and incompetent and not very threatening, despite their occasional sheeted displays. The KKK was the largest anti-Semitic group in the U.S. in those days, he told us, not saving its hatred only for African-Americans but also for Catholics and Jews.

"But today there are thousands of tiny underground neo-Nazi, skinhead and Klan organizations which are completely organized and disciplined, and each one is a time bomb," he said. "They thrive in the secrecy of computer boards. Each one is independent and has its own goals. If they ever get together — the way Gerlock was uniting the neo-Nazi groups — we're in for real trouble."

He also told us about the Michigan Militia, six thousand strong, the largest states' rights organization in the country, headquartered right in the Upper Peninsula and Northern Michigan in some of those backwoods log cabins and isolated mobile homes that dot the lush green countryside. Probably in some of those rich brick ranch homes too.

Tess's car and Kitt's suitcase were never found. Lamppa and Gerlock said Rudy had been responsible for anything of that matter. Probably Rudy left the Blazer on the side of the highway with the keys in it. Gerlock never revealed another name of his followers. So they're still out there, leaderless — for the moment. Maybe until Rudy's great-grandchildren and their friends get out of high school.

Gerlock said Rudy's primary motive was loyalty to the memory of the deceased man he'd served for sixty years. Even though Rudy had gone back to Germany to serve during World War II, for which Gerlock had admired him greatly, he'd never truly "caught the spirit," Hank said. When Rudy finagled his way illegally back into the U.S. later, he turned into a robot for the Frederich Wilhelm Tessels, both I and II. "Rudy was old, he had no vision." Gerlock with a sneer dismissed his former right-hand man.

No one else in Beer Barrel could be connected to their efforts in any way. But I suspect that other members of Gerlock's group are out there, waiting for us to return in the spring.

Tess finally admitted that it would be impossible to pull off a large-scale music festival this summer, so we'll see. We're making steps on setting up the grant program for lesbian musicians, writers and artists, however. She's pretty sure that she will go on as scheduled. Once we can pin down all her ideas and dreams.

One of the women who found out about the grants even before they were announced wrote to us for an application blank. She suggested that we call the lodge "Sofia Center for the Arts," since Sofia, also spelled Sophia, was considered the greatest goddess of all. She is the wisdom goddess, the "Mother of God the Creator," this writer said, "and an apt leader for artists seeking wisdom and truth through creative efforts." Tess loved the name and declared her lodge renamed as of that instant. The grant program will also be administered through the newly created nonprofit Sofia Foundation.

At some point Tess is going to be the recipient of hundreds of thousands of copies of anti-Semitic propaganda, once the trials are over. At first she said she was going to make a giant bonfire, but Kitt came up with the idea of donating it to one of the Holocaust museums. Probably the Detroit museum, since Ford had been such a Michigan icon. Kitt examined my copy of *The International Jew* and remembered that her parents had shown her a copy when she was a child.

"Our temple bought reprints from the National Council of Christians and Jews as part of a campaign to keep the lessons of the Holocaust alive," Kitt said. "Now it's time for another generation to see this shit."

Tess traced Henry Ford's name on the cover of the booklet with her finger. "In all my research I never learned Ford was so blatantly anti-Semitic."

"Yeah, my folks boycotted all Ford products for a

long time," Kitt said. "I'm a little older than you —
as the years pass, everything is forgotten. When Ford
died, his grandsons did so much for the Jewish
community to try to compensate for old Henry that
finally the boycott died out."

Kitt read some more from the booklet and kept
shaking her head. "The grandson sold Ford Motor
Company products cheaply to Israel when the country
was first getting started, when no one else would. So
the company lost billions in sales from Arab
countries. Today my dad drives a Lincoln, enough
said?"

One of the FBI agents who lingered on mop-up
detail was Burt Fisher, an expert on hate crimes,
particularly the neo-Nazi movement. He sat with us
in front of the fireplace one afternoon and gave us
more background.

Despite bundles of clothes, Fisher was pencil-thin.
His angular face was Michigan ashen, and his short
black crewcut was almost repeated in his five o'clock
shadow. With my L.A. frame of reference I thought
at first he was on some kind of speed, but I soon
realized his super-charged enthusiasm reflected his
extreme interest in his subject.

He told us incredible stories about Henry Ford,
who grew up in an age when the only Jews he'd
seen were itinerant peddlers. "He only finished
seventh grade, but because he was an industrial giant
people paid attention to everything he said."

Fisher's favorite story was of the time *The
Chicago Tribune* editorially called Ford an ignorant
fool. "So Ford sued the paper for a million dollars.
On the stand, Ford said that he *thought* there had
been an American revolution in the year eighteen-

twelve. He said Benedict Arnold was 'a writer — I think,' and he defined *chile con carne* as 'a large, mobile army.' " Fisher glanced up to see if we were smiling, as he was.

"The jury found Ford had indeed been libeled but only awarded him six cents. So he decided to buy his own newspaper to get his views across." Ford purchased a little country newspaper called *The Dearborn Independent* and built the cost of a subscription into the purchase price of every Model T. At one point he had a million subscribers.

For ninety-one weeks straight, the paper published a series of anti-Semitic articles which were later reprinted, bundled into four booklets, and sold separately as *The International Jew.* One of the articles was "The Protocols of the Elders of Zion," a phony document written by a czarist sympathizer in Russia to deflect an uprising by blaming Jews. "This piece is particularly vicious," Burt said. "It never seems to die."

Years and decades later, *The International Jew* was still circulating throughout the world, particularly Europe and Latin America, Burt said, "always with Ford's photo and signature to give it authority. He deliberately had no copyright placed on the articles so that they could be reprinted by anyone."

Groups that did included the Ku Klux Klan, the National States Rights Party, and The John Birch Society. "Apparently old man Tessel did his bit to keep it circulating too." Burt made a vague motion in the direction of the attic where the boxes of copies had been found.

"Did anybody really pay attention to this shit?" Kitt asked.

"Hitler cited *The International Jew* in *Mein Kampf,* and the leader of Hitler's Youth Movement testified during the Nuremberg trials that he became anti-Semitic after reading the booklet."

Everybody, even the last most dedicated FBI agent, rushed to finish by Christmas eve. Kitt used all of her influence to get us tickets to L.A. in this heaviest of all air traffic periods.

I drove Kitt and Tess to the Ironwood airport to catch their shuttle and decided that instead of joining them, I'd fly out of Detroit Metro. Even though it meant spending Christmas day in some motel in the middle of nowhere. Christmas hasn't been an important holiday for me since I left Anne's house. At the end of the drive to the airport I'd turn in the rented Jeep. This time on the way, I'd take the I-75 turn-off to Rochester.

CHAPTER TWENTY-ONE

Patrick Malone lived in a well-landscaped, yellow brick two-story home on a cul-de-sac in suburban Detroit. A chain-link fence enclosed the entire property, the reason for which I saw immediately: a golden retriever puppy which had the run of the place, yapping like a fool.

"Hi, pup," I said, bending over to receive my share of licks and pawing. Inside the fence the snow was packed down to the moldering grass by pawprints; outside, the city was blanketed by a fresh three inches, on its way to becoming slush in the streets as the post-Christmas rush-hour traffic pummeled it with dirt.

I gave thanks again for the four-wheel-drive that had carried me through the city with nary a slide, while all around me cars had careened out of control. By now everybody should have relearned how to drive in snow, but some people never learn. The cold snap had continued to the lower peninsula, enveloping most of the Midwest in a deep freeze, the worst winter anyone could remember.

Heidi Malone came to the door in response to the puppy's commotion and welcomed me inside. "You're Laney Samms! I recognize you from TV. Down, pup! We're raising him to be a leader dog," she explained. Patrick was an executive with Leader Dogs for the Blind, Hayley had told me.

He had been blinded by an overuse of oxygen at birth, back when the only way doctors knew to save the lives of premature infants was with high doses of oxygen, doses that too often slipped over the elusive "safe" range and burned the corneas of the saved babies.

Today scientists know about things like surfactant, a kind of liquid detergent that lines the lungs of babies and keeps them open, and which can be added artificially to the lungs of preemies born without enough.

Heidi and Patrick were a few years younger than Hayley's forty-three, though their settled suburban lifestyle made them appear much older than the former rock star. Heidi had on jeans and an expensive embroidered version of a blue work shirt that set off her ash blonde hair — too evenly one color throughout to be natural.

Patrick had just come home from work and wore a charcoal suit that matched his hair and a light blue Oxford shirt and silk tie that matched his eyes. He was thin like Hayley, while Heidi tended to middle-age spread. She wore her shirttails out and her jeans unbelted. Both had kind faces. This was a good place for Hayley.

I noticed that instead of a leader dog he used a fold-up white cane kept in his pocket. "Heidi drives me everywhere, and I know my way around the house and the office, so I don't need a dog," he explained.

"We like to keep a pup around though. With both our kids away at school, we've got plenty of time. Leader dogs need a loving family setting for their first year, and we do give them that, don't we, honey?" The pup bounded back and forth between its owners.

"I've got to change," he said to me, trying to keep the wet pup off his suit. "Hayley's upstairs — I'll get her."

The house inside followed a sophisticated gray and pale yellow color scheme, with pale ash wood tables and cabinets, though the gray carpet was commercial-strength tweed and the wrap-around sofa and recliner were a matching hardy fabric resistant to puppy paws. The Malones' tree was an artificial blue pine, with non-breakable foil and straw ornaments on the lower branches where the pup grazed the tree in its sprints. The house held few other signs of the holiday season.

When Hayley appeared at the top of the stairs, Heidi excused herself to join her husband, taking the romping pup with her.

Hayley descended the ash wood staircase like a debutante in white, though instead of a formal dress she wore white leggings and sweat shirt, and her white-socked feet were shoeless. Her face was almost as white as her clothes. No eye makeup today. There was something institutional about all that white. It seemed appropriate. She seemed like a patient in a mental hospital, not quite in focus.

Hayley had shaved her head again; for her it wasn't a fashion statement. She'd taken the razor to her white scalp during her fourth stay in Betty Ford Center as a symbol of starting a new life. She'd told me that the drug treatment program Synanon had shaved addicts' heads routinely as a sign of entering a new life, and sometimes as a punishment.

So now she was starting yet another new life. Had she been through nine already, I wondered? The feisty kid of her childhood had died when she'd started to keep secrets, big ones, and every time that child had tried to reemerge, the clamp had come down once more.

"Can I get you a Diet Pepsi?" She moved awkwardly toward the hall to the kitchen instead of entering the living room where I sat, deep in the wrap-around sofa. "I want one myself."

"In that case, okay." I waited until she reemerged with two cans.

"Do you need a glass?"

"Of course not." She sat down awkwardly across from me. Finally I broke the silence, trying to be light and friendly. "How the heck are you, Hayley?"

"Oh, I've been better. I'm in therapy now. With a psychiatrist at Henry Ford Hospital. A woman. She specializes in substance abuse." Hayley reached to her scalp with a probing finger, patting a red spot that must have been a razor nick. Her face grimaced when she touched the cut.

"Good," I said, sipping my soda. "Do you like her?"

"That doesn't much matter, does it? The question is, can she help me?"

"I think you have to like someone you're in therapy with. At least I'd have to like someone before I could open up to them."

"Yeah, I like her." Hayley drained her can in one nervous chug-a-lug. She put the can on the floor where it tipped over and dribbled its last drops on the carpet. Diet Pepsi doesn't stain, I hoped. The Malones kept this house spotless despite the pup.

"Look, I ... have to apologize for the way I behaved at the lodge," she started. "I don't know what came over me. Suddenly ... I couldn't handle it anymore."

"I gathered that. It's okay. Everything turned out okay in the end." I tried to bring her up-to-date on the legal cases and on what I had learned about Henry Ford's influence on the Tessel lodge, but she didn't seem to hear any of it, so I stopped. Somehow I hadn't expected her to seem so sick, so out of it.

"I tried to get back into the Betty Ford Center, but they had a long waiting list, and they said I hadn't followed orders after my other stays," Hayley said. "But they recommended this psychiatrist." She looked at me with ice cool eyes. Like ice cubes that were melting fast.

"That's good. How often do you see her?"

"My health insurance is still paying for it, so I go three times a week. Did I ever tell you how my mother put all my early earnings into a trust fund with automatic insurance deductions, so that I'd have enough money to live on all my life? She did that for me before she died."

"Yes, you told me." Hayley's mother had committed suicide shortly after her daughter became a success. Today doctors would call her mother's disease manic-depression, or bi-polar disorder, and they'd treat it with lithium carbonate. Back then lithium was still experimental, and she'd died too soon.

"You once said a therapist told you that you might have inherited a tendency toward your mother's manic-depression — is your psychiatrist checking that out?"

"Yeah, she did. She agrees, but she doesn't think I need lithium. She thinks I can learn to handle crises better with more therapy. She's trying a new drug on me too." Hayley slipped a brown plastic pill bottle from her pocket and tossed it to me.

I didn't recognize the drug name, another of those garbled syllable soups that drug companies make up that bear no resemblance to either the chemical in the medicine or the illness the drug is to treat.

"It makes me a little sleepy. She says it takes a few weeks to achieve full effect."

"To be honest, I didn't realize you were this sick, Hayley. Otherwise, I don't think I would have . . ."

Fucked your brains out from the moment you stepped off the plane.

"I wasn't. I mean, I didn't think I was either. It was all that tension over the kidnapping. I flipped, that's all. Just like I did all the other times. Figuring out what had happened in my past didn't automatically mean I was cured, and I thought it did."

"I guess I did too. Makes sense. You took a few months off to try to get your head together..." She'd disappeared into this safe haven before, and I'd thought she'd emerged when she was ready to face life again.

"It wasn't enough time. And I didn't get help. I didn't even go to an AA meeting all that time I was here before. I just sat in my room and thought about how I was well, I had no more reason to act out, I could do anything now. I was wrong. I'm sorry..." And she broke into tears and sobbed into her arm. I moved over next to her and rubbed her back and said comforting words. Eventually she stopped.

"I can't be in a relationship with someone who is still drinking, and you're not in any kind of place to be in a relationship yourself," I finally said, when she'd sniffled and found a Kleenex box and sat upright in her chair again and looked me in the eyes. My words sounded too harsh the moment I uttered them. But then my mission this trip had been to break off with her, only I'd said the words too fast.

"You're right." Hayley stared forlornly at a bas-relief wall hanging of stampeding horses, done in black and gold. We were both silent for a long time.

"You ought to go back to Anne," she finally said.

Her words startled me, shook me. "I tried, remember? Anne said it was too late, it was over for good," I replied when I could.

"Maybe." Hayley managed a weak smile in my direction. "If not Anne, then somebody else. Somebody stable. No more rock stars."

"Uh huh," I said. I thought about an old Stones

song lyric, something to that fact that maybe I really had been looking for a lunatic. We made idle chit-chat to cover our discomfort, and then Heidi came downstairs to invite me to stay for dinner. I apologized and said my good-byes. "I wish you a good life and a speedy treatment, and I will always remember you with warm feelings," I whispered to Hayley in our farewell hug.

She merely rolled her eyes again and told me, "Get out of here already."

Dinner was a drive-through Whopper and fries. A florist was open late and I sent a cheery bouquet to be delivered the next day.

Leaving Detroit, I felt relieved, which I'd expected, and sad, which I'd also expected, but I also felt good. Not like the last time Hayley and I had said our good-byes. She was finally getting ongoing treatment, and I had hopes she would be okay.

I'm not real clear about the relationship between mental illness and drinking — when I'd tried therapy I kept finding more and more excuses for why I drank, but never the strength to finally quit. Not until AA. I hoped Hayley wasn't going the wrong direction. Curing an alcohol and drug dependency with more drugs? But that was her problem, her decision. If there was some biochemical problem that pills could cure, more power to her.

I felt as if I'd grown a lot the past few months — and if you don't grow up at age fifty, when the hell are you going to get around to it?

Though my original goals for organizing Tess's music festival had hardly turned out the way I'd planned, I could actually say I was proud of the way I'd handled myself. I could indeed handle pressure and challenge, and then some. My ego had to be a few feet higher after this experience.

Looking back even further, I had to admit that I had done the right thing by breaking up with Anne, even though it had meant leaving the safety of almost twenty years in one relationship, and incurring the wrath of almost everyone in the community. I'd never grown up, and I wouldn't have, clinging to her protection. Life was good. Life was wide open for new things to come.

I couldn't wait to get home to the routine of L.A. Peace and quiet — funny to think of L.A. in terms of peace and quiet. And warmth! I couldn't wait to get out of all these clothes. Back in cut-offs, Radar at my side, maybe Flirt on my pillow, if I could convince Kitt we needed a mouser in the guest house. The hot tub and pool. My PR clients to reestablish contact with and work out new plans. The bar to check on, though Carmen was undoubtedly handling things just fine. A new class at UCLA Extension. The quiet, stable life of Los Angeles.

AFTERWORD

Lisa Edwards, rabbi of Beth Chayim Chadshim Temple in Los Angeles, helped me to see how Hanukkah might be celebrated today by a lesbian feminist.

Lesbian Connection "Contact Dyke" Nissa Annakindt gave me a great deal of information about life in the Upper Peninsula, both the lesbian community and Finn culture.

Jann Hillenbrand and Teri Solinger from St. Cloud, Minnesota, soulmates from the Michigan Womyn's Music Festival, were great companions as we explored the Upper Peninsula ourselves looking for locations for this novel.

Louis Davis, president emeritus of Beth Tephilath Moses Synagogue in Mount Clements, Michigan, shared his personal memories of the Michigan Jewish community's reactions to Henry Ford's anti-Semitism and to the Henry Ford v. *The Chicago Tribune* trial in Mount Clemens in 1919, and he pointed me in the right research directions.

My source in the military, who would rather not be named in a lesbian novel in these days of "Don't ask, don't tell," no matter what his orientation, gave me information about guns, car bombs, paintball, sabot shells, and numerous other technical matters.

The assistance of the above people has been invaluable; any errors in my interpreting and presenting their information are my own.

As always, Norma Hair is my first-line editor and major plot supplier, and she deserves but will not accept a joint byline. She is also responsible for teaching me that history is not bunk. Christine Cassidy also provided excellent editorial direction.

For those who wish to learn more about Henry Ford's anti-Semitism and the propaganda booklet *The International Jew,* many books are available. Particularly valuable in my research were *The Fords: An American Epic,* by Peter Collier and David Horowitz (New York: Summit Books, 1987); *The Public Image of Henry Ford,* by David L. Lewis (Detroit: Wayne State University, 1976); and *Ford: We Never Called Him Henry,* by Harry Bennett as told to Paul Marcus (New York: Tom Doherty Associates, Inc., 1951, 1987).

The advertisement for "The Israeli Challenge Training Program" cited in Chapter Nineteen is from the March, 1995 issue of *Soldier of Fortune* magazine, whose pages are insightful reading for feminists.

A few of the publications of
THE NAIAD PRESS, INC.
P.O. Box 10543 • Tallahassee, Florida 32302
Phone (904) 539-5965
Toll-Free Order Number: 1-800-533-1973
Mail orders welcome. Please include 15% postage.

CABIN FEVER by Carol Schmidt. 256 pp. Sizzling suspense
and passion. ISBN 1-56280-089-1 $10.95

THERE WILL BE NO GOODBYES by Laura Dehart Young. 192
pp. Romantic love, strength, and friendship. ISBN 1-56280-103-1   10.95

FAULTLINE by Sheila Ortiz Taylor. 144 pp. Joyous comic
lesbian novel. ISBN 1-56280-108-2   9.95

OPEN HOUSE by Pat Welch. 176 pp. P.I. Helen Black's fourth
case. ISBN 1-56280-102-3   10.95

ONCE MORE WITH FEELING by Peggy J. Herring. 240 pp.
Lighthearted, loving romantic adventure. ISBN 1-56280-089-2   10.95

FOREVER by Evelyn Kennedy. 224 pp. Passionate romance — love
overcoming all obstacles. ISBN 1-56280-094-9   10.95

WHISPERS by Kris Bruyer. 176 pp. Romantic ghost story
ISBN 1-56280-082-5   10.95

NIGHT SONGS by Penny Mickelbury. 224 pp. A Gianna
Maglione Mystery. Second in a series. ISBN 1-56280-097-3   10.95

GETTING TO THE POINT by Teresa Stores. 256 pp. Classic
southern Lesbian novel. ISBN 1-56280-100-7   10.95

PAINTED MOON by Karin Kallmaker. 224 pp. Delicious
Kallmaker romance. ISBN 1-56280-075-2   9.95

THE MYSTERIOUS NAIAD edited by Katherine V. Forrest &
Barbara Grier. 320 pp. Love stories by Naiad Press authors.
ISBN 1-56280-074-4   14.95

DAUGHTERS OF A CORAL DAWN by Katherine V. Forrest.
240 pp. Tenth Anniversay Edition. ISBN 1-56280-104-X   10.95

BODY GUARD by Claire McNab. 208 pp. A Carol Ashton Mystery.
6th in a series. ISBN 1-56280-073-6   9.95

CACTUS LOVE by Lee Lynch. 192 pp. Stories by the beloved
storyteller. ISBN 1-56280-071-X   9.95

SECOND GUESS by Rose Beecham. 216 pp. An Amanda Valentine
Mystery. 2nd in a series. ISBN 1-56280-069-8   9.95

THE SURE THING by Melissa Hartman. 208 pp. L.A. earthquake
romance.   ISBN 1-56280-078-7   9.95

A RAGE OF MAIDENS by Lauren Wright Douglas. 240 pp. A
Caitlin Reece Mystery. 6th in a series.   ISBN 1-56280-068-X   9.95

TRIPLE EXPOSURE by Jackie Calhoun. 224 pp. Romantic drama
involving many characters.   ISBN 1-56280-067-1   9.95

UP, UP AND AWAY by Catherine Ennis. 192 pp. Delightful
romance.   ISBN 1-56280-065-5   9.95

PERSONAL ADS by Robbi Sommers. 176 pp. Sizzling short
stories.   ISBN 1-56280-059-0   9.95

FLASHPOINT by Katherine V. Forrest. 256 pp. Lesbian
blockbuster!   ISBN 1-56280-043-4   22.95

CROSSWORDS by Penny Sumner. 256 pp. 2nd Victoria Cross
Mystery.   ISBN 1-56280-064-7   9.95

SWEET CHERRY WINE by Carol Schmidt. 224 pp. A novel of
suspense.   ISBN 1-56280-063-9   9.95

CERTAIN SMILES by Dorothy Tell. 160 pp. Erotic short stories.
                                            ISBN 1-56280-066-3   9.95

EDITED OUT by Lisa Haddock. 224 pp. 1st Carmen Ramirez
Mystery.   ISBN 1-56280-077-9   9.95

WEDNESDAY NIGHTS by Camarin Grae. 288 pp. Sexy
adventure.   ISBN 1-56280-060-4   10.95

SMOKEY O by Celia Cohen. 176 pp. Relationships on the
playing field.   ISBN 1-56280-057-4   9.95

KATHLEEN O'DONALD by Penny Hayes. 256 pp. Rose and
Kathleen find each other and employment in 1909 NYC.
                                            ISBN 1-56280-070-1   9.95

STAYING HOME by Elisabeth Nonas. 256 pp. Molly and Alix
want a baby . . . or do they?   ISBN 1-56280-076-0   10.95

TRUE LOVE by Jennifer Fulton. 240 pp. Six lesbians searching
for love in all the "right" places.   ISBN 1-56280-035-3   9.95

GARDENIAS WHERE THERE ARE NONE by Molleen Zanger.
176 pp. Why is Melanie inextricably drawn to the old house?
                                            ISBN 1-56280-056-6   9.95

KEEPING SECRETS by Penny Mickelbury. 208 pp. A Gianna
Maglione Mystery. First in a series.   ISBN 1-56280-052-3   9.95

THE ROMANTIC NAIAD edited by Katherine V. Forrest &
Barbara Grier. 336 pp. Love stories by Naiad Press authors.
                                            ISBN 1-56280-054-X   14.95

UNDER MY SKIN by Jaye Maiman. 336 pp. A Robin Miller
mystery. 3rd in a series.   ISBN 1-56280-049-3   10.95

STAY TOONED by Rhonda Dicksion. 144 pp. Cartoons — 1st
collection since *Lesbian Survival Manual.*   ISBN 1-56280-045-0   9.95

CAR POOL by Karin Kallmaker. 272pp. Lesbians on wheels
and then some!   ISBN 1-56280-048-5   9.95

NOT TELLING MOTHER: STORIES FROM A LIFE by Diane
Salvatore. 176 pp. Her 3rd novel.   ISBN 1-56280-044-2   9.95

GOBLIN MARKET by Lauren Wright Douglas. 240pp. A Caitlin
Reece Mystery. 5th in a series.   ISBN 1-56280-047-7   10.95

LONG GOODBYES by Nikki Baker. 256 pp. A Virginia Kelly
mystery. 3rd in a series.   ISBN 1-56280-042-6   9.95

FRIENDS AND LOVERS by Jackie Calhoun. 224 pp. Mid-western
Lesbian lives and loves.   ISBN 1-56280-041-8   10.95

THE CAT CAME BACK by Hilary Mullins. 208 pp. Highly
praised Lesbian novel.   ISBN 1-56280-040-X   9.95

BEHIND CLOSED DOORS by Robbi Sommers. 192 pp. Hot,
erotic short stories.   ISBN 1-56280-039-6   9.95

CLAIRE OF THE MOON by Nicole Conn. 192 pp. See the
movie — read the book!   ISBN 1-56280-038-8   10.95

SILENT HEART by Claire McNab. 192 pp. Exotic Lesbian
romance.   ISBN 1-56280-036-1   10.95

HAPPY ENDINGS by Kate Brandt. 272 pp. Intimate conversations
with Lesbian authors.   ISBN 1-56280-050-7   10.95

THE SPY IN QUESTION by Amanda Kyle Williams. 256 pp.
4th Madison McGuire.   ISBN 1-56280-037-X   9.95

SAVING GRACE by Jennifer Fulton. 240 pp. Adventure and
romantic entanglement.   ISBN 1-56280-051-5   9.95

THE YEAR SEVEN by Molleen Zanger. 208 pp. Women surviving
in a new world.   ISBN 1-56280-034-5   9.95

CURIOUS WINE by Katherine V. Forrest. 176 pp. Tenth Anniversary Edition. The most popular contemporary Lesbian love story.
                                                     ISBN 1-56280-053-1   10.95
          Audio Book (2 cassettes)   ISBN 1-56280-105-8   16.95

CHAUTAUQUA by Catherine Ennis. 192 pp. Exciting, romantic
adventure.   ISBN 1-56280-032-9   9.95

A PROPER BURIAL by Pat Welch. 192 pp. A Helen Black
mystery. 3rd in a series.   ISBN 1-56280-033-7   9.95

SILVERLAKE HEAT: A Novel of Suspense by Carol Schmidt.
240 pp. Rhonda is as hot as Laney's dreams.   ISBN 1-56280-031-0   9.95

LOVE, ZENA BETH by Diane Salvatore. 224 pp. The most talked
about lesbian novel of the nineties!   ISBN 1-56280-030-2   10.95

A DOORYARD FULL OF FLOWERS by Isabel Miller. 160 pp.
Stories incl. 2 sequels to *Patience and Sarah.*   ISBN 1-56280-029-9   9.95

MURDER BY TRADITION by Katherine V. Forrest. 288 pp. A
Kate Delafield Mystery. 4th in a series. ISBN 1-56280-002-7 9.95

THE EROTIC NAIAD edited by Katherine V. Forrest & Barbara
Grier. 224 pp. Love stories by Naiad Press authors.
                                  ISBN 1-56280-026-4 13.95

DEAD CERTAIN by Claire McNab. 224 pp. A Carol Ashton
mystery. 5th in a series. ISBN 1-56280-027-2 9.95

CRAZY FOR LOVING by Jaye Maiman. 320 pp. A Robin Miller
mystery. 2nd in a series. ISBN 1-56280-025-6 9.95

STONEHURST by Barbara Johnson. 176 pp. Passionate regency
romance. ISBN 1-56280-024-8 9.95

INTRODUCING AMANDA VALENTINE by Rose Beecham.
256 pp. An Amanda Valentine Mystery. First in a series.
                                  ISBN 1-56280-021-3 9.95

UNCERTAIN COMPANIONS by Robbi Sommers. 204 pp.
Steamy, erotic novel. ISBN 1-56280-017-5 9.95

A TIGER'S HEART by Lauren W. Douglas. 240 pp. A Caitlin
Reece mystery. 4th in a series. ISBN 1-56280-018-3 9.95

PAPERBACK ROMANCE by Karin Kallmaker. 256 pp. A
delicious romance. ISBN 1-56280-019-1 9.95

MORTON RIVER VALLEY by Lee Lynch. 304 pp. Lee Lynch
at her best! ISBN 1-56280-016-7 9.95

THE LAVENDER HOUSE MURDER by Nikki Baker. 224 pp.
A Virginia Kelly Mystery. 2nd in a series. ISBN 1-56280-012-4 9.95

PASSION BAY by Jennifer Fulton. 224 pp. Passionate romance,
virgin beaches, tropical skies. ISBN 1-56280-028-0 10.95

STICKS AND STONES by Jackie Calhoun. 208 pp. Contemporary
lesbian lives and loves. ISBN 1-56280-020-5 9.95
Audio Book (2 cassettes) ISBN 1-56280-106-6 16.95

DELIA IRONFOOT by Jeane Harris. 192 pp. Adventure for Delia
and Beth in the Utah mountains. ISBN 1-56280-014-0 9.95

UNDER THE SOUTHERN CROSS by Claire McNab. 192 pp.
Romantic nights Down Under. ISBN 1-56280-011-6 9.95

GRASSY FLATS by Penny Hayes. 256 pp. Lesbian romance in
the '30s. ISBN 1-56280-010-8 9.95

A SINGULAR SPY by Amanda K. Williams. 192 pp. 3rd
Madison McGuire. ISBN 1-56280-008-6 8.95

THE END OF APRIL by Penny Sumner. 240 pp. A Victoria
Cross mystery. First in a series. ISBN 1-56280-007-8 8.95

HOUSTON TOWN by Deborah Powell. 208 pp. A Hollis
Carpenter mystery. ISBN 1-56280-006-X 8.95

KISS AND TELL by Robbi Sommers. 192 pp. Scorching stories
by the author of *Pleasures*. ISBN 1-56280-005-1   10.95

STILL WATERS by Pat Welch. 208 pp. A Helen Black mystery.
2nd in a series. ISBN 0-941483-97-5   9.95

TO LOVE AGAIN by Evelyn Kennedy. 208 pp. Wildly romantic
love story. ISBN 0-941483-85-1   9.95

IN THE GAME by Nikki Baker. 192 pp. A Virginia Kelly
mystery. First in a series. ISBN 1-56280-004-3   9.95

AVALON by Mary Jane Jones. 256 pp. A Lesbian Arthurian
romance. ISBN 0-941483-96-7   9.95

STRANDED by Camarin Grae. 320 pp. Entertaining, riveting
adventure. ISBN 0-941483-99-1   9.95

THE DAUGHTERS OF ARTEMIS by Lauren Wright Douglas.
240 pp. A Caitlin Reece mystery. 3rd in a series.
ISBN 0-941483-95-9   9.95

CLEARWATER by Catherine Ennis. 176 pp. Romantic secrets
of a small Louisiana town. ISBN 0-941483-65-7   8.95

THE HALLELUJAH MURDERS by Dorothy Tell. 176 pp. A
Poppy Dillworth mystery. 2nd in a series. ISBN 0-941483-88-6   8.95

SECOND CHANCE by Jackie Calhoun. 256 pp. Contemporary
Lesbian lives and loves. ISBN 0-941483-93-2   9.95

BENEDICTION by Diane Salvatore. 272 pp. Striking, contemporary romantic novel. ISBN 0-941483-90-8   9.95

BLACK IRIS by Jeane Harris. 192 pp. Caroline's hidden past . . .
ISBN 0-941483-68-1   8.95

TOUCHWOOD by Karin Kallmaker. 240 pp. Loving, May/
December romance. ISBN 0-941483-76-2   9.95

COP OUT by Claire McNab. 208 pp. A Carol Ashton mystery.
4th in a series. ISBN 0-941483-84-3   9.95

THE BEVERLY MALIBU by Katherine V. Forrest. 288 pp. A
Kate Delafield Mystery. 3rd in a series. ISBN 0-941483-48-7   10.95

THAT OLD STUDEBAKER by Lee Lynch. 272 pp. Andy's affair
with Regina and her attachment to her beloved car.
ISBN 0-941483-82-7   9.95

PASSION'S LEGACY by Lori Paige. 224 pp. Sarah is swept into
the arms of Augusta Pym in this delightful historical romance.
ISBN 0-941483-81-9   8.95

THE PROVIDENCE FILE by Amanda Kyle Williams. 256 pp.
Second Madison McGuire ISBN 0-941483-92-4   8.95

I LEFT MY HEART by Jaye Maiman. 320 pp. A Robin Miller
Mystery. First in a series. ISBN 0-941483-72-X   9.95

THE PRICE OF SALT by Patricia Highsmith (writing as Claire
Morgan). 288 pp. Classic lesbian novel, first issued in 1952 . . .
acknowledged by its author under her own, very famous, name.
ISBN 1-56280-003-5   9.95

SIDE BY SIDE by Isabel Miller. 256 pp. From beloved author of
Patience and Sarah.   ISBN 0-941483-77-0   9.95

STAYING POWER: LONG TERM LESBIAN COUPLES by
Susan E. Johnson. 352 pp. Joys of coupledom. ISBN 0-941-483-75-4   14.95

SLICK by Camarin Grae. 304 pp. Exotic, erotic adventure.
ISBN 0-941483-74-6   9.95

NINTH LIFE by Lauren Wright Douglas. 256 pp. A Caitlin Reece
mystery. 2nd in a series.   ISBN 0-941483-50-9   8.95

PLAYERS by Robbi Sommers. 192 pp. Sizzling, erotic novel.
ISBN 0-941483-73-8   9.95

MURDER AT RED ROOK RANCH by Dorothy Tell. 224 pp.
A Poppy Dillworth mystery. 1st in a series.   ISBN 0-941483-80-0   8.95

LESBIAN SURVIVAL MANUAL by Rhonda Dicksion. 112 pp.
Cartoons!   ISBN 0-941483-71-1   8.95

A ROOM FULL OF WOMEN by Elisabeth Nonas. 256 pp.
Contemporary Lesbian lives.   ISBN 0-941483-69-X   9.95

THEME FOR DIVERSE INSTRUMENTS by Jane Rule. 208 pp.
Powerful romantic lesbian stories.   ISBN 0-941483-63-0   8.95

CLUB 12 by Amanda Kyle Williams. 288 pp. Espionage thriller
featuring a lesbian agent!   ISBN 0-941483-64-9   8.95

DEATH DOWN UNDER by Claire McNab. 240 pp. A Carol
Ashton mystery. 3rd in a series.   ISBN 0-941483-39-8   9.95

MONTANA FEATHERS by Penny Hayes. 256 pp. Vivian and
Elizabeth find love in frontier Montana.   ISBN 0-941483-61-4   8.95

LIFESTYLES by Jackie Calhoun. 224 pp. Contemporary Lesbian
lives and loves.   ISBN 0-941483-57-6   9.95

WILDERNESS TREK by Dorothy Tell. 192 pp. Six women on
vacation learning ''new'' skills.   ISBN 0-941483-60-6   8.95

MURDER BY THE BOOK by Pat Welch. 256 pp. A Helen Black
Mystery. First in a series.   ISBN 0-941483-59-2   9.95

THERE'S SOMETHING I'VE BEEN MEANING TO TELL YOU
Ed. by Loralee MacPike. 288 pp. Gay men and lesbians coming out
to their children.   ISBN 0-941483-44-4   9.95

LIFTING BELLY by Gertrude Stein. Ed. by Rebecca Mark. 104 pp.
Erotic poetry.   ISBN 0-941483-51-7   8.95

AFTER THE FIRE by Jane Rule. 256 pp. Warm, human novel by
this incomparable author.   ISBN 0-941483-45-2   8.95

THREE WOMEN by March Hastings. 232 pp. Golden oldie. A
triangle among wealthy sophisticates.   ISBN 0-941483-43-6   8.95

PLEASURES by Robbi Sommers. 204 pp. Unprecedented
eroticism.   ISBN 0-941483-49-5   8.95

EDGEWISE by Camarin Grae. 372 pp. Spellbinding
adventure.   ISBN 0-941483-19-3   9.95

FATAL REUNION by Claire McNab. 224 pp. A Carol Ashton
mystery. 2nd in a series.   ISBN 0-941483-40-1   8.95

IN EVERY PORT by Karin Kallmaker. 228 pp. Jessica's sexy,
adventuresome travels.   ISBN 0-941483-37-7   9.95

OF LOVE AND GLORY by Evelyn Kennedy. 192 pp. Exciting
WWII romance.   ISBN 0-941483-32-0   8.95

CLICKING STONES by Nancy Tyler Glenn. 288 pp. Love
transcending time.   ISBN 0-941483-31-2   9.95

SOUTH OF THE LINE by Catherine Ennis. 216 pp. Civil War
adventure.   ISBN 0-941483-29-0   8.95

WOMAN PLUS WOMAN by Dolores Klaich. 300 pp. Supurb
Lesbian overview.   ISBN 0-941483-28-2   9.95

THE FINER GRAIN by Denise Ohio. 216 pp. Brilliant young
college lesbian novel.   ISBN 0-941483-11-8   8.95

OCTOBER OBSESSION by Meredith More. Josie's rich, secret
Lesbian life.   ISBN 0-941483-18-5   8.95

BEFORE STONEWALL: THE MAKING OF A GAY AND
LESBIAN COMMUNITY by Andrea Weiss & Greta Schiller.
96 pp., 25 illus.   ISBN 0-941483-20-7   7.95

OSTEN'S BAY by Zenobia N. Vole. 204 pp. Sizzling adventure
romance set on Bonaire.   ISBN 0-941483-15-0   8.95

LESSONS IN MURDER by Claire McNab. 216 pp. A Carol
Ashton mystery. First in a series.   ISBN 0-941483-14-2   9.95

YELLOWTHROAT by Penny Hayes. 240 pp. Margarita, bandit,
kidnaps Julia.   ISBN 0-941483-10-X   8.95

SAPPHISTRY: THE BOOK OF LESBIAN SEXUALITY by
Pat Califia. 3d edition, revised. 208 pp.   ISBN 0-941483-24-X   10.95

CHERISHED LOVE by Evelyn Kennedy. 192 pp. Erotic Lesbian
love story.   ISBN 0-941483-08-8   9.95

These are just a few of the many Naiad Press titles — we are the oldest and
largest lesbian/feminist publishing company in the world. Please request a
complete catalog. We offer personal service; we encourage and welcome
direct mail orders from individuals who have limited access to bookstores
carrying our publications.